PUFFIN BOOKS

THE CHRISTMASAURUS
AND THE
WINTER WITCH

THE CHRISTMASAURUS
AND THE
WINTER WITCH

TOM FLETCHER

Illustrations by Shane Devries

PUFFIN

PUFFIN BOOKS

UK | USA | Canada | Ireland | Australia
India | New Zealand | South Africa

Puffin Books is part of the Penguin Random House group of companies
whose addresses can be found at global.penguinrandomhouse.com.

www.penguin.co.uk   www.puffin.co.uk   www.ladybird.co.uk

First published 2019
002

Cover, illustrations and text copyright © Tom Fletcher, 2019
Illustrations by Shane Devries
The moral right of the author has been asserted

Set in Baskerville MT Pro
Text design by Mandy Norman
Printed in Great Britain by Clays Ltd, Elcograf S.p.A.

A CIP catalogue record for this book is available from the British Library

HARDBACK
ISBN: 978–0–241–33852–0

INTERNATIONAL PAPERBACK
ISBN: 978–0–241–33853–7

All correspondence to:
Puffin Books, Penguin Random House Children's
80 Strand, London WC2R 0RL

For Mum & Dad.
Thanks for always making Christmas magical.

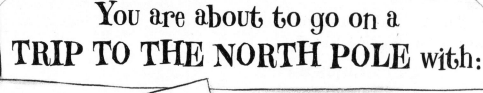

You are about to go on a
TRIP TO THE NORTH POLE with:

William Trundle
who loves dinosaurs.

Brenda Payne
who used to be naughty but now she's nice.

Pamela Payne
Brenda's mum, who has promised to try her best to like Christmas this year.

Bob Trundle
William's dad, who still LOVES Christmas.

The one and only, should-be-extinct, flying, roaring, friendly, soaring **Christmasaurus!**

The most magically massive, massively magical man in the universe: **Santa!**

They're always merry, always rhyming, minuscule with perfect timing . . . it's **Santa's elves!**

And someone so mysterious, so top-secret, that I can't believe her name is on the cover of this book . . . **The Winter Witch!**

Oh, and before I forget, watch out for this snooty-looking chap: **Barry Payne.** He might be trouble in the future . . .

CONTENTS

PROLOGUE
THE FUTURE

This story starts like all good stories do, *a long time ago . . .*

What do you mean, *that's how the first book started?*

No, it isn't! OK, I'll check. Hang on . . .

Well, what do you know? You're right!

We can't have that. I'll change it.

How's this . . .

This story starts totally, completely, ginormously differently to the first book, *a long time in the future!*

You didn't see *that* coming, did you, smartypants?

The future isn't much different from the now. Future

kids still go to school every day. And, yes, future kids still have to eat broccoli and peas. And brush their teeth. And say please and thank you. And wash their future belly buttons. And not pick their future noses. (Or eat future bogeys.)

None of those things have changed in the future.

There is, however, one absolutely whopping great big difference.

In the future, there is

NO CHRISTMAS!

I KNOW, RIGHT!

Let's take a look . . .

It was a totally ordinary winter's evening in the future. Super-awesome flying cars were whizzing overhead on the skyway that weaved in and out of the stratospheric starscrapers (buildings so tall that their tips tickled the beginning of outer space!), and a soft sprinkling of snow was settling across future London.

All of a sudden, the snowfall began to thicken. It didn't thicken evenly all over the city, though, as you'd expect. Quite the opposite, in fact. It began to snow heavily in one very small, very precise spot on a quiet little alleyway called Thistle Lane.

In just a few seconds, the snowfall was so heavy it began to pile up on top of itself, creating what looked like a mini-mountain. Then, just as suddenly as it had started, it stopped, leaving a big white mound of snow in the middle of the lane.

Puff!

A fist popped out of the snow pile. Then . . . *puff!* Another fist!

Next, this two-armed pile of snow began to shake and wobble until it fell to the ground, revealing a young boy with curly brown hair, his wheelchair covered in dinosaur stickers.

You know him already, of course.

William Trundle rubbed his forehead and looked around the quiet street.

'Hello? Where am I? No . . . *WHEN* am I?' he asked – because William wasn't alone in Thistle Lane. Beside him in the shadows of the alleyway stood a mysterious figure.

But there was no reply. All the strange figure did was raise its arm and point one cold, slender finger at the end of Thistle Lane.

Frowning, William quietly wheeled himself down the empty alley and turned out on to the main road.

This was William's first look at *the future*!

The air was glowing with brilliant, blinding light blasting from enormous screens that lined the sides of the starscrapers.

The tallest building, at the very centre, was topped with a colossal, dazzling letter **P** that eclipsed the moon and appeared to dominate the city.

William tried to take in the bizarre sights and smells of future London, wanting to remember every detail:

* *the people wearing smart future suits, busily walking to work*
* *the traffic jam of flying cars looming over the city*
* *the twenty-decker buses with robot bus conductors.*

There was so much to see. But William's concentration was interrupted by whispering voices behind him. He turned and peered further down the alleyway.

'Hello?' he called out.

There was no reply, but the strange figure, who was still waiting quietly in the shadows, nodded once. William moved back along Thistle Lane, until he realized that the voices he could hear were *singing*.

> '*There's no time like Christmas,*
> *It's the best time of year.*
> *Oh, how we miss it –*
> *Now it fills us with fear . . .*'

'*Fear?*' whispered William. 'Did I just hear that right?' Silently, he moved himself towards the strange singing and peered past a rubbish bin. A group of people were huddled together round a small fire. They were wrapped up warm, in big overcoats and woolly hats.

One of them, a kind-looking old man with wrinkled rosy cheeks, unzipped his overcoat, proudly revealing a fluffy knitted Christmas jumper as though he were setting it free.

The rest of the group followed suit, unzipping and unbuttoning their coats to share their brilliantly festive jumpers underneath as they continued to sing:

> '*We won't stop believing,*
> *It's the only way*
> *That anyone will ever*
> *See another Christmas Day.*'

A chilly breeze whooshed down the shadowy lane, picking up rubbish. A newspaper floated through the air like a kite, and came to rest by William's feet. He peered down at it and read the date.

'December the twenty-fifth? This is Christmas Day –

in thirty years' time?' he whispered, scrunching up his face as he turned back to the busy main street.

Why are people going to work on Christmas Day? William wondered.

Then he saw that none of the buildings had decorations. None of the people looked merry. None of the street lamps had those tacky lights twisting up them that William's dad, Bob, loved so much. In fact, if it hadn't been for the secretive carollers down that dark alley, it wouldn't have felt like Christmas at all!

Suddenly red twinkly lights lit up the alley and warmed the faces of the secret carollers.

Ah, that's more Christmassy! William thought.

'They're here!' the wrinkly rosy-cheeked caroller cried, pointing a shaky finger at something zooming towards them. And William realized the red lights weren't fairy lights at all. They were the blinding red flashing lights of a flying police car!

'It's the CP! They've found us – run!' another caroller shouted, zipping up his coat to hide his jumper.

The CP? Who on earth are they? William wondered as he reversed his wheelchair further behind the bin and hid.

PROLOGUE

The doors of the flying police car hissed open, and a squad of officers leapt down from the vehicle.

'Christmas Police, freeze!' one of the officers boomed through a megaphone while his partners sprang into action, chasing after the covert carollers, who ran into the darkness of Thistle Lane.

All except one. The old man.

'I won't be scared any more,' the rebel Christmas caroller said defiantly, removing his coat to reveal the loudest, fluffiest, Christmassiest Christmas jumper William had ever seen.

'Sarge, I think that's a musical jumper . . .' the officer said nervously as they closed in on the caroller.

'Put your arms where we can see 'em,' barked the sergeant as she and her squad surrounded the man.

The caroller didn't budge.

'I said, arms where we can see 'em. Nice and slow,' the commanding officer repeated.

'We didn't do anything wrong!' the caroller protested.

'The rules and regulations of the *Christmas Ban* have been made perfectly clear.'

William stared.

Christmas Ban?

Suddenly the old caroller squeezed the knitted bauble in the centre of his Christmas jumper.

'NO!'

'Cover your ears!'

'GRAB HIM!' the officers cried – but it was too late. The baubles came to life with flashes of red and green, and a burst of song echoed through the alleyway.

'Jingle bells, jingle bells, jingle all the way . . .'

It lasted for the briefest of moments before the officers tackled the old man to the snowy ground and cuffed him.

'You'll never ban Christmas!' he cried.

'Oh, not that again,' groaned the sergeant.

'You know this one?' asked another officer.

'Know him? Since the Christmas Ban, he's spent more Christmases behind bars than he has in his own bed. You just can't let Christmas go, can you, Bob Trundle?'

The words seemed to echo in William's brain:

Bob . . .

Bob . . .

BOB...

Trundle . . .

Trundle . . .

TRUNDLE...

'**DAD!**' William blurted out from his hiding place, then quickly clapped his hands over his mouth. His dad was too busy being bundled into the back of the police car to hear his time-travelling son call out – but the sergeant wasn't.

'Who said that?' she barked, turning to look in William's direction. 'You there! Are you another caroller?'

One of the officers began running towards William. He knew he had to move – and fast – but he couldn't help but stare at the old, wrinkly, future version of his father in handcuffs in the back of the police car as the officers slammed the door shut. And all because he sang a Christmas carol and wore a Christmas jumper!

'Something has gone horribly wrong!' William whispered.

PROLOGUE

The officer was fast approaching. 'Take me back!' William cried to the mysterious figure that had suddenly appeared beside him in the shadows. 'Take me back now!'

This strange creature instantly raised its icy hand and reached out of the darkness to clasp the push handles of William's 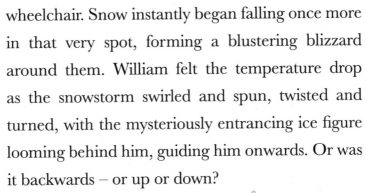 wheelchair. Snow instantly began falling once more in that very spot, forming a blustering blizzard around them. William felt the temperature drop as the snowstorm swirled and spun, twisted and turned, with the mysteriously entrancing ice figure looming behind him, guiding him onwards. Or was it backwards – or up or down?

William wasn't sure.

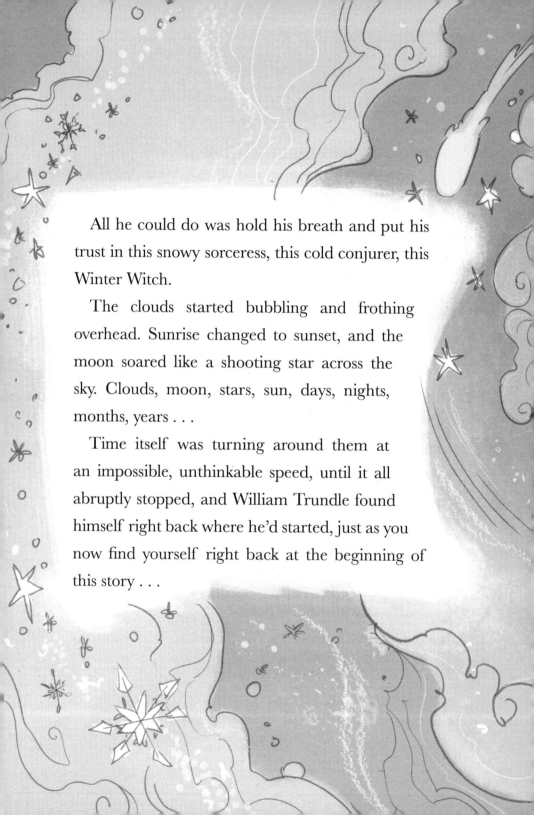

All he could do was hold his breath and put his trust in this snowy sorceress, this cold conjurer, this Winter Witch.

The clouds started bubbling and frothing overhead. Sunrise changed to sunset, and the moon soared like a shooting star across the sky. Clouds, moon, stars, sun, days, nights, months, years . . .

Time itself was turning around them at an impossible, unthinkable speed, until it all abruptly stopped, and William Trundle found himself right back where he'd started, just as you now find yourself right back at the beginning of this story . . .

CHAPTER ONE

THE BEGINNING OF THIS STORY

'**M**erry first day of the Christmas holidays, William!'

William Trundle opened his eyes as Pamela Payne carefully stepped into his bedroom with a breakfast tray wobbling in her hands. 'Oh . . . morning!' he said sleepily, propping himself up on his dinosaur pillow.

'Your dad made the pancakes,' Pamela explained as she set the tray in front of him, trying not to spill any more orange juice than she already had. 'Just how you like them, apparently.'

16

THE BEGINNING OF THIS STORY

William looked down and saw the stack of steaming yumminess wafting up warm smells of vanilla and cinnamon.

'**Mmmmm**, *vaninnamon!*' he said, smiling.

'Sorry?'

'Vanilla and cinnamon . . . *vaninnamon!* It's what Dad calls it,' William explained, picking up his knife and fork and tucking in.

'Oh, I see! That's very *Bob.*' Pamela smiled.

'Where *is* Dad?' William asked. But his question was answered by a cheerful knock on the bedroom door next to his.

'Wakey-wakey, Brenda! It's the start of the Christmas holidays! Time for pancakes and orange juice. It's a Trundle Christmas Tradition!' sang Bob Trundle from out in the hallway, followed by the click of Brenda's bedroom door opening.

'No school *and* pancakes! Yes!' cheered Brenda's muffled voice from the next room.

'Your dad said that now that Brenda and I live here, we have to experience the *Trundle Christmas Traditions*,' Pamela explained, putting on her best *Bob* voice.

William grinned. 'Well, I hope you're ready for the most Christmassy Christmas EVER!' he said through a mouthful of pancake.

'You know what, I think that's just what Brenda needs.'

'What about you?' William said.

'Oh, I'll try my best,' said Pamela, smiling. 'But I am **not** wearing one of those awful Christmas jumpers!'

William frowned. 'Oh, but Dad has already got you a musical one, with lights and everything . . .'

Pamela paused for a moment and William saw a flash of festive fear in her eyes.

'I'm kidding!' he said with a grin.

Pamela breathed a sigh of relief and they both laughed.

'When you've finished your breakfast, your dad said to make your way to the kitchen for your advent calendar.'

THE BEGINNING OF THIS STORY

And, with that, Pamela left William alone to enjoy his breakfast – but he wasn't alone for long. A few moments later, William heard a little creak from the hallway, and out of the corner of his eye he noticed his bedroom door opening a peek.

'I know you're there, Brenda. You are literally *the worst* at spying on people,' William said, not even looking up from his plate.

'Not fair! I'm great at spying. I've just not lived here long enough to figure out where all the creaky floorboards are yet!' Brenda huffed. She waltzed in with her breakfast tray and plonked herself down on William's bed, making herself comfortable.

'This is awesome!' she said, shoving her last huge slice of syrup-covered pancake into her mouth. 'How many Trundle Christmas Traditions are there?'

William smiled. 'Well, *today* it's mince pies. Dad and I always make them on the first day of the school holidays! Then we can decorate our bedrooms with the leftover tinsel Dad couldn't fit in the living room. And before bed we'll watch a Christmas movie. Maybe two if there's time!'

Brenda shook her head.

'What?' asked William.

'I just never imagined having Willypoos as a brother would actually be so awesome.'

'It's *step*brother!' William replied.

PAUSE STORY!

Yep, you heard that correctly. William and Brenda referred to themselves as *stepbrother and sister*! And that's because they were!

Sort of.

If you cast your brains back to last Christmas, you may remember that Bob Trundle and Pamela Payne – William's dad and Brenda's mum – were swept away with the magic of Christmas morning and danced in the snowy street as Santa flew into the sky, after an evil hunter was gobbled up by a flying dinosaur. (It's a long story – literally!)

Well, that Christmas magic didn't want to leave them and, in the summer, Bob and Pamela decided that the Paynes would move in with the Trundles! It *was* a bit of a squeeze in their wonky little house, and sometimes William wondered if he'd ever get used to it. It had been just him and his dad for a very long time, after all.

Now back to this Christmas . . .

Brenda stared up at the dinosaur wallpaper that covered every inch of William's bedroom walls.

Above his desk he had a corkboard covered with drawings and pieces of artwork. All of them were of the same thing: a blue flying dinosaur, with shimmering scales and a frosty mane of icicles.

For William, this was the most magical thing to happen to him last Christmas – in fact, it was the most magical thing to happen to him ever! Meeting his best friend: the Christmasaurus.

'Do you think we'll see him again this year?' Brenda asked.

'I hope so!' William said wistfully. 'I miss that dinosaur!'

Brenda suddenly sat up, gazing at the sky through William's bedroom window.

'What is it?' William asked excitedly, trying to see what Brenda was looking at.

'Is that . . . *him*?' she gasped, pointing to the clouds.

William scanned the snowy sky, desperate to see if it was really him. Had the Christmasaurus come to visit him early?

Brenda burst out laughing, her mouth full of food, and William turned round to see that the last piece of pancake was missing from his plate.

'Oh, you are **SO** back on that Naughty List,' William told her, feeling a tiny pang of disappointment. Seeing the Christmasaurus again was all he had been hoping for, all year long.

'What? This is exactly what big sisters are for.' Brenda shrugged as she hopped off the bed.

'How many times do I have to tell you? You are not my *big* sister. We're the SAME AGE!' William replied as he slipped his dinosaur-patterned jumper on and transferred into his wheelchair, which was waiting by the bed.

'I'm a month older than you, so technically I *am* your big sister.' Brenda wrapped her fluffy pink cardigan around herself as they headed out of the bedroom together.

THE BEGINNING OF THIS STORY

'If you want to get "technical", you're not my sister at all!' William protested. 'Our parents aren't married.'

'*Yet!* But they're living together, so it's just a matter of time. It's what grown-ups do: *kiss, move in with each other, get married, argue.*'

'Morning, Willypoos!'

William's dad smiled as William and Brenda came into the kitchen. Pamela was sipping a cup of tea, and William felt a little pang in his heart as he saw which cup she'd chosen – the glistening blue teacup with a snowflake-shaped handle.

'Oh,' he said. 'That was . . . That teacup belonged to . . .'

Pamela froze.

'Oh, William, I'm sorry. I've done it again, haven't I?' she said, quickly putting the pretty cup down. 'I totally forgot that one belonged to . . . well, that it was special.'

'No, it's OK,' William said. He knew he was being a bit silly about the whole thing, but it was such a strange feeling, seeing Pamela with something that had belonged to his mum.

He remembered when his dad had thought about donating it to charity. 'It's only a cup, Willypoos,' he'd said softly. But William wasn't quite ready to let it go, even though he'd never actually seen his mum drinking from it. He was so young when she died that he could barely remember her, but just knowing that she'd once held it in her hands seemed like reason enough to keep it.

He saw his dad give Pamela a reassuring smile before clearing his throat.

'Right, everyone. Now it's time for the second Trundle Christmas Tradition of the day – washing up,' Bob said, throwing snowflake-patterned tea towels to William and Brenda, and grinning as Brenda's face fell.

Once the pans and plates were tidied away, Bob slid William's and Brenda's advent calendars across the kitchen table and they quickly set to work finding door number fourteen.

'Found it!' William yelled, opening the little cardboard door.

'Me too!' said Brenda a second later, shoving the chocolate into her mouth.

26

THE BEGINNING OF THIS STORY

'Only ten days until Christmas!' William said excitedly.

Brenda stared at him. 'Oh no!' she said. 'It's December the fourteenth – that means that Dad's coming to pick me up today!'

She slumped in her seat, and William saw a glimpse of the old, sulky Brenda. 'Urgh! It's so unfair that I have to stay with *him* this Christmas!' she huffed.

'Do you *have* to?' William asked.

'I'm afraid so, William,' said Pamela. 'Brenda's dad and I agreed that she would alternate Christmases, and she was with me last year, so . . .'

'Dad's place it is!' Brenda sighed.

A sad silence fell on the kitchen for a moment.

'Not to worry!' Bob chimed merrily. 'We'll just have to make the most of every second that you are here today! The four of us celebrating Christmas together, the Trundle way!' He picked up a beautiful snow globe from the table, which had a hand-carved wooden base and a small, cosy-looking log cabin inside the glass ball. He turned it over and the snow swirled around, creating a magical scene. 'We'll make mince pies, sing songs, roast chestnuts . . .'

'And crumpets, Dad – don't forget the crumpets!' William added as he and Brenda watched the snow settling on the miniature house inside the snow globe.

'And crumpets! Well remembered, William. Oh, we'll have enough fun today to last you all Christmas, Brenda, don't you worry about that. And, if Christmas with your dad really is as bad as you think, then it will be over in the blink of an eye, it always is, and then we can start looking forward to next year, when we'll all be together. The four of us.'

There was a loud bark from beneath the kitchen table.

'*Five* of us! Sorry, Growler,' Bob corrected himself, and reached down to give their adopted dog a pat on his scruffy head.

'You'll be back home before you know it, Brenda. And, if I've said it once, I've said it a thousand times: every second away from one Christmas . . .'

'. . . is one second closer to the next!' they all joined in, and burst out laughing.

'That's more like it. Keep smiling, Brenda. It's Christmas!' Bob said, before launching into a solo rendition of 'The Twelve Days of Christmas'.

THE BEGINNING OF THIS STORY

'Your dad can't be *that* bad, can he?' William asked quietly as Bob began twirling Pamela around the kitchen.

'Well, you know how your dad is fun, loves Christmas, always tells the truth, checks how you're feeling, knows what your favourite things are, tells you that he loves you . . .'

They both looked at Bob, who was still singing, and had now slipped on a pair of fake antlers.

'Yeah!' said William.

'And do you remember when we had "opposites day" at school and had to imagine that everything was the other way round? Up was down, left was right, in was out . . . good was bad?'

'Yep.'

'Well, my dad is like your dad on opposites day!' Brenda explained, opening door number fifteen of her advent calendar and popping the chocolate into her mouth.

'Oh,' William said, thinking that now was probably not the time to tell her she shouldn't do that.

'Plus, I haven't seen him for almost a year. And that's not all.' Brenda took a deep breath. 'Before my dad comes to pick me up, there's something you should know about him . . .'

But just as Brenda was about to tell William . . .

Her voice disappeared.

That's right!

Vanished!

Gone!

Vamoosed!

Her lips were moving, but it was as though someone had accidentally leant on the mute button and switched off her sound.

'What? I can't hear you!' William said. Or at least he tried to – but his voice had disappeared too!

They both looked around and realized that the entire kitchen was absolutely silent, as if something had sucked out all the sound. There was no gush of running water from the sink, no carol from Bob's mouth, not a single jingle of a bell from his jumper!

The Beginning of This Story

It was even quieter than quiet. Like someone had turned the volume down on William's ears and when the volume reached zero had just kept going into minus-quiet.

That's when William noticed something else a little fishy, a little out of the ordinary, a little . . . magical. Through the kitchen window, a flock of pigeons that had just taken flight were floating absolutely still in mid-air, as if they'd been stunned by a freeze-ray that had glued them to the air itself.

Snowflakes had also stopped mid-fall and were hanging in the air as though suspended by invisible string from the sky. Growler was stuck mid-bark at the window. In fact, the only things that *were* moving were William, Brenda, Bob and Pamela!

Bob turned round, leaving the mug he was holding floating in the air. Pamela shrieked at the strange sight, but no sound came out.

This is weird! William thought to himself as he went to the window and peered out at the perfectly still morning. He saw Yusuf next door suspended in mid-jump above his trampoline and an aeroplane hovering in one spot in the sky. Even the second hand on the kitchen clock wasn't tick-tocking, as though – by some kind of magic – time itself were frozen!

A smile started to grow on William's face – he couldn't stop it.

What is it? Brenda mouthed, wondering why William suddenly looked so excited.

William was excited because he had seen this kind of magic once before. He knew that there was only one person in the whole world who could make something like this happen. Someone who was about to land in the next chapter . . .

SANTA!

CHAPTER TWO
REUNITED

An enormous **BOOM** rumbled down from the clouds above.

'Look!' William shouted, his voice suddenly coming back as he pointed at the sky.

The sky lit up with a flash of lightning, and out of the clouds burst a resplendent red sleigh, in an explosion of music and environmentally friendly glitter. It was pulled by nine utterly magnificent creatures, who galloped on the air as though it were as solid as the tiles underneath William's wheels. Eight of these creatures were, as you would expect, Magnificently Magical Flying Reindeer

– but the creature that led the herd was a little more impossible.

A little more extinct.

A little more *the title of this book* . . .

The Christmasaurus!

His shimmering blue scales sparkled like stars and his galloping claws clipped the wisps of clouds. He soared across the sky as though he had wings – but of course the Christmasaurus didn't need wings to fly.

He had William's belief.

REUNITED

'Ho, ho, ho!' boomed the jolliest voice in the world, and the Christmasaurus let out an excited roar as he banked hard to his right and brought the sleigh down into the Trundles' garden for a perfect landing.

Well, perfect as long as you don't count totally taking out next-door's fence and crashing through Yusuf's football net, before flattening their garden shed and clopping hoofprints into Bob's vegetable patch.

The sleigh skidded to a stop on the snowy patio and silence fell across the frozen garden.

'Blimey, that landing was quite, er, something! Ho, ho!' chuckled Santa as he got to his feet and straightened his red velvet hat. He snapped his fingers and, just like that, the big trail of mess they'd created un-messed itself. The hoofprints popped back to snowy perfection. The carrots and turnips in the vegetable patch replanted themselves. The football net jumped back on to its frame, and the wooden planks of the garden shed flew back neatly into place. All was back to normal.

'Santa!' William called excitedly as he, Brenda, Bob and Pamela rushed out of the back door. William wheeled himself over to the enormous sleigh, but, before he could get there, a large, dinosaur-shaped lump of blue landed on his lap.

'Christmasaurus!' William laughed as the scaly dinosaur slurped at his face like an excited puppy. 'I've missed you too!'

The Christmasaurus let out a happy chirp and wagged his tail. It had been almost a whole year since they'd shared an unthinkable adventure and become best friends, and William was so happy to see that the

Christmasaurus had missed him as much as he'd missed the Christmasaurus.

'William Trundle!' Santa interrupted with a jolly smile as he nimbly slid down the bonnet of his sleigh and then performed a fancy forward roll across the patio. For such a large man, Santa was very athletic.

'Christmas crackers, you've grown up since last year, William! Must be all the sprouts your father is feeding you, eh, Bobble? Bring it in for a hug, you old chestnut! And of course I remember you, Pamela Payne. Looking a little jollier this year, I must say! And where's that ex-Naughty Lister? There she is! Blinking baubles, Brenda, that is a bright cardigan, ho, ho! Wonderful to see you all looking so . . . together!' Santa said, barely taking a breath as he greeted them all excitedly.

Bob stood gawping at the magical sight in front of him with teardrops sparkling in his eyes. 'G-g-good to see you again, Santa!' he spluttered, and Pamela quickly put her arm round him, helping snap him back into the moment.

William went over to Santa and wrapped his arms round his fat-tastic belly (which indeed shook when he laughed, but was more like a bowl full of thick custard than jelly). Hugging Santa was like hugging a great friendly polar bear, and he was as warm as a fresh mug of hot chocolate.

'What are you doing here? It's not Christmas yet!' he asked.

'William, that's no way to greet His Merriness,' Brenda said in a strange voice that sounded like she was doing a bad impression of the Queen. 'How marvellous to make your acquaintance once again, Mr Claus,' she added, curtsying so low that her curly hair brushed the snow.

'Why are you talking like that?' William asked.

'Like what, William?' she said quickly. 'One doesn't know what you mean.'

'Like *that*!' William said.

'Brenda, Brenda, Brenda!' Santa chuckled. 'You don't have to try so hard to seem nice. Nice isn't a performance, it's a . . . it's a . . . well, nice is nice! And besides, I've been monitoring you all year and you're certainly heading for another year on the Nice List.'

Brenda punched the air with her fists. 'YES! HA! Knew it! Eat that, Willypoos, you big . . .' She paused. Santa was watching her with both bushy white eyebrows raised. 'You big . . . brilliant . . . boy?' she finished, roughing up William's hair and grinning sheepishly.

Santa burst into a booming laugh that made his shoulders bounce up and down. 'Bob, Pamela, Brenda and . . . *Willypoos? Do they really still call you that?*' he whispered to William.

William blushed. 'Well, yes, but . . .'

'And Willypoos! Well, butter my crumpets, it feels so good to be back here with you, but I've not come all this way just for a visit.' Santa beamed cheekily, and William could see that he was enjoying himself. 'No, no! I've come to bring you all back to visit *me*. At the North Pole!'

The family was silent.

Stunned.

'Well, we were hoping for a little bit more of a reaction than that, weren't we!' Santa beamed at the Christmasaurus, who wagged his tail.

'You mean *us*?' Bob said hopefully, pointing to himself and the family.

'Yes!' Santa replied.

'Go with you?'

'Correctmas!'

'To the North Pole?'

'Abso-cringle-utely!'

'On *that*?' Bob asked, indicating the glistening sleigh.

'Bingo Crosby! Well, unless you have another magical vehicle that can transcend time and space and transport you to the North Pole in a matter of seconds . . . *yes*, on that!' Santa laughed. 'Now you may have noticed that time is indeed frozen, and it won't stay that way forever, so if you'd be so kind as to board the sleigh . . .'

40

REUNITED

'But we haven't arranged a dog-sitter for Growler!' Brenda said, glancing at her frozen pet, who was paused mid-bark at the kitchen window.

'Not to worry! You'll be back in the twitch of a moustache. He won't even know you've gone,' said Santa with a smile.

William watched as his dad stepped over to the sleigh and ran a shaking hand along the glistening golden skis that curled up at the front into enormous loops.

'Magical,' Bob whispered.

'If you think that's magic, Dad, wait until you fly in it!' William said as a ramp magically lowered for him and he wheeled himself up into the sleigh, and Brenda climbed up after him.

'But . . . why are you taking us to the North Pole?' Pamela asked, carefully stepping in after Bob.

William thought he saw the hint of a shadow flit across Santa's face, just for a nanosecond. Then the jolly man seemed to shake it off, and he was beaming brightly once again.

'Well, that's a very good question. You see, I don't get many visitors and, as much as I enjoy the elves'

company, they can be a little bit . . . er, a teeny bit . . . erm, how can I say it . . . really . . .'

'Merry?' William suggested.

'*VERY!*' Santa said. 'And so I thought it would be fun to show some human folk around. Since William already came last year, and you all saw me, as clear as day out in the street, I decided that if anyone was going to come up and visit, it should be you lot! A tour of the North Pole – my treat! And, of course, the Christmasaurus has been longing to see you again, William,' he added, and the dinosaur let out a happy roar.

'This is already better than last Christmas!' Brenda said happily.

Well, Brenda, this story has only just begun. You won't believe your perfectly twirly hair when all the time travel starts, and then there's the Winter Witch and – Sorry, no spoilers!

'Now, Bob, did you by any chance keep hold of that candy cane I gave you last year?' Santa asked.

'Keep it? It's not left his sight!' Pamela laughed as Bob pulled something out from underneath his Christmas jumper; it was tied around his neck with red ribbon.

'Right here!' Bob smiled, holding the shimmering

red-and-white candy cane in the air.

'Good! You're going to need that! Christmasaurus, ready?' Santa boomed.

The Christmasaurus slipped his head into the lead harness and let out a puff of warm air through his nostrils.

'Reindeer?' Santa bellowed.

They replied by shaking themselves like eight wet dogs, making their jingle bells jangle.

'William, Bob, Brenda, Pamela, are *you* ready?' Santa asked with a smile.

'YES!'

'Then I hope you know the words . . .'

From somewhere within his bottomless pockets, Santa pulled out a whopping great golden gramophone and a gleaming record. He slipped the record on the turntable, and a triumphant fanfare of trumpets suddenly blasted from the ornate brass horn. The sleigh instantly lifted away from the patio, floating on a cushion of sound that seemed to project into the air ahead of them, showing the Christmasaurus and the reindeer the way like a path made of music in the sky.

'To the NORTH POLE!' Santa cried and, as they

flew over the Trundles' wonky little house, he began to sing:

'Into the sky on Santa's sleigh,
To the North Pole and back again.
No one will know we've been away
Because we're frozen in time.

Going to see where Santa lives,
Watch the elves wrap the toys he gives.
Seeing how magical it is
When we're frozen in time.'

'We're **FLYING!** We're actually flying!' Bob screamed, unable to contain his excitement any longer – which only seemed to lift the sleigh higher.

The Christmasaurus glanced back from the front of the herd of flying reindeer and caught William's eye. William gave him a nod, and with a happy roar the Christmasaurus charged up into the wintry sky.

If the rest of the town hadn't been frozen in time,

people would have seen the most bizarre sight. I mean,
it's not every morning you see a family flying in the
back of Santa's sleigh behind eight magical reindeer
and a dinosaur.

'Look, William, there's our school!' Brenda said,
pointing down at the tiny playground below.

'And that's Freddie's house!' William said, spotting
their classmate's rooftop.

'Ah yes, the tall young chap at number twenty-eight. Fantastic little mince pie he left me last year!' Santa shouted back from behind the reins.

'And there's Lola's house!' cried Brenda excitedly, spotting the home of another of their friends below.

'Right you are! Any chance you could ask her parents to reposition those outdoor lights on her roof? They got awfully tangled in the deers' antlers a couple of years ago – took hours to untangle,' Santa said.

William stared down in wonder at the twisting and turning streets below. Somehow the town looked more magical from above.

'Are we there yet?' asked Brenda, breaking the silence. 'I could do with a wee . . .'

'We've not even left London, Brenda!' said Santa.

Silence fell as the sleigh sailed a few clouds further along the sky, but after a few moments Santa started fidgeting in his seat.

'Oh, cringlesticks! Now you've made me need the loo too!' he said. 'We'll make a quick stop at the services, and then we're not stopping again until we get to the North Pole!'

He steered the sleigh down into the nearest motorway services, where they all popped to the loo (including the Christmasaurus and the eight Magnificently Magical Flying Reindeer – and, yes, they also do Magnificently Magical Poops). William gazed around at the people, all of whom were frozen in time too.

The people filling up their cars with fuel: **frozen**.

The people buying coffee and cheese toasties and sausage rolls: **frozen**.

The people waiting for the breakdown van: **frozen**.

It was like walking through a photograph.

Once they were all done and feeling a little lighter, they took their places back on the sleigh.

'Righty-ho, all aboard and ready to fly – to the North Pole and into the sky!' Santa boomed, turning up the music once again as the Christmasaurus led them beyond the clouds.

CHAPTER THREE

WELCOME TO THE NORTH POLE

All was quiet at the North Pole.

Mountains of ice towered over the pure white snow that blanketed the vast expanse of emptiness.

To the casual observer, it would appear that there was nothing here. That's because, to see Santa's North Pole Snow Ranch, you have to be invited.

Lucky for you then that Santa has allowed me to give you all your very own Cosmos-Converting Candy Cane.

Here you go:

OK, this is just a drawing, so it's probably best you don't eat it – but its magic is no less powerful.

'Bob?' Santa called back as the sleigh began to descend. 'Time to see if that candy cane is past its best-before date!'

Bob took a deep, trembly breath, and then bit off a chunk of the magical treat before handing it to Pamela. She crunched off a piece too and passed it to Brenda, who snapped it in two, shoved one half in her mouth and gave the other to William.

As William looked at it, the candy cane's snapped sugary edges sparkled like peppermint stardust, and he couldn't resist. He popped it in his mouth, and a gloriously minty tingle spread through him.

'You might want to have a peep below,' Santa called

back to them, smiling, and the four passengers leant over the edge of the sleigh to see the first twinkling lights of the North Pole begin to emerge.

'I can see it!' Bob squeaked.

As they watched the lights, Santa softly spoke these words:

'Imagine all your wildest dreams
Together in one place.
The dreams that make you wake up
With a smile upon your face,

Swimming in a sea of sweets,
Or floating like a cloud.
And, as you dream, your favourite song
Is playing nice and loud.

You may think that this dream
Is not a place that you can go,
But if you think like that
Then it's a place you'll never know.

THE CHRISTMASAURUS AND THE WINTER WITCH

The wonders of your dreams
Are never right in front of you.
Until you wish it to exist
A dream cannot come true.

So now that you are dreaming
Try to hold on nice and tight,
And maybe, if we wish it would come true,
Then it just might . . .'

While his dad, Pamela and Brenda all looked down at the magic unfolding below, William thought the most magical thing of all was right up there in the sky with them. He looked ahead at the Christmasaurus, a shimmering blue flash bobbing up and down as he galloped along the dancing lights of the aurora borealis that seemed to surround the sleigh in warmth, like an invisible hug.

'You might want to hold on tight – that dinosaur friend of yours still hasn't quite got the hang of landing yet!' Santa laughed, slipping some snow goggles down from the fluffy brim of his hat to cover his eyes.

WELCOME TO THE NORTH POLE

William heard the sound of the Christmasaurus's claws clicking on ice, followed by the clop of reindeer hooves, and finally the swish of the sleigh's golden skis as they slid across the snow.

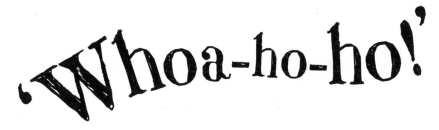

'Whoa-ho-ho!'

Santa called, pulling hard on the reins while the Christmasaurus dug his claws into the snow – but the sleigh was still travelling too fast. It suddenly started to spin round and round in great circles – until they finally came to a halt.

Everything was silent.

The landing had kicked up a cloud of snow that shrouded the sleigh in a white mist, so that its passengers couldn't see anything surrounding them.

'Everyone all right back there?' Santa laughed heartily. 'We're still working on stopping, but the Christmasaurus will get the hang of it by Christmas Day, I'm sure.

Anyway, you'll be glad to know that we're here! We've arrived! So off we pop then. We've got all the time in the world, but it doesn't mean we should dilly-dally.'

Santa leapt from the front of the sleigh and cartwheeled into the white fog, humming merrily as he disappeared.

'I can't believe I'm actually back at the North Pole!' Bob whispered shakily. 'I never thought I'd EVER see this place again!'

'**Look!**' William interrupted, excitedly pointing at several small, shadowy figures appearing through the snowy mist.

'Argh! What are they?!' cried Brenda.

'You don't need to be afraid. They're elves!' William beamed. 'Hello, elves!'

At that very moment, the figures stepped out of the mist.

It was Snozzletrump, Specklehump, Sparklefoot, Sugarsnout, Starlump, Snowcrumb, Spudcheeks and . . . er . . . what was the other one called again?

Oh yes, Sprout!

Welcome to the North Pole

These were the eight elves who had discovered the Christmasaurus many years ago.

'William! William! Welcome back!
We're so pleased you're here.
We've got so much to tell you
About what's happened this past year!'

they chimed in perfect unison as the ramp magically lowered and William wheeled himself down from the sleigh.

'Yes, yes, yes, we'll have time for all that later!' Santa stomped back through the mist towards them, bringing a huge crowd of excited elves with him. 'But first I believe a little welcome performance has been planned for you all.'

At that, the crowd of elves leapt to attention and cleared a path for a single elf to step forward. William didn't recognize him. He was shabby and tired-looking, wearing a dark, floor-length coat and a beret. He wore dark glasses and smelt of strong coffee.

'Children, allow me to introduce Starcloth, head of

entertainment at the North Pole.' Santa grinned.

'Is he OK?' William whispered to Santa.

'Oh yes, yes, yes, he's fine. He's just been working tirelessly to put this show together for you all. Bit of a perfectionist is Starcloth,' murmured Santa. 'Takes it all very seriously.'

'Oooh, a show! Is it a panto?' asked Pamela.

There was a nervous gasp from the elves, and William thought Starcloth looked very upset. 'A *panto*! I'm a serious artiste,' he snapped.

WELCOME TO THE NORTH POLE

'No, no, not a *panto*,' Santa whispered, covering Starcloth's ears for a moment. 'It's a sort of welcome ceremony. Starcloth wrote it, choreographed it, directed it and is starring in it! When you're ready, Starcloth.' Santa gave the dishevelled elf a nudge.

Starcloth took a deep breath and closed his eyes. Then, suddenly, he whipped off his coat and hat, while twirling once on the spot. When he stopped, his clothes had been transformed into an outfit of shimmering sparkles and stars. In his hand appeared a glittery microphone, and he began to sing:

'There's nowhere on the planet like the
   North Pole,
A diamond in the northern Arctic sea,
But never trust an elf just cos he says so.
If you believe, then you will start to see . . .

There's nowhere on the planet like the North Pole.
It's everything you want a place to be.
Just avoid the snow if it is yellow
Cos that's the place the reindeer like to pee.

There's nowhere on the planet like the North Pole.
We don't rehearse the harmonies.
Everything you see exists when you believe
In the N.O.R.T.H. P.O.L.E.'

On his final note, the other elves surrounding the children twirled on the spot – and revealed sparkly costumes too! William stared as, from the snowy mist around them, there emerged an orchestra of snowmen playing carrot flutes and plucking pine cones, a group of cheerleading Arctic foxes spelling the words

NORTH POLE

with their bushy tails, an aerobatic display from the forest fairies, crumpet jugglers, twenty tap-dancing polar bears and a partridge in a pear tree. Sprout and Starlump performed a quickstep, while Sugarsnout played the drums on Snozzletrump's very round bottom.

The elves joined Starcloth in his song:

'Welcome to the North Pole, William.
You can make yourselves at home.
There's nowhere else on Earth this brilliant,
Here you'll never sing alone.

Welcome to the North Pole, William.
It's wilder than your wildest dreams.
It's not a case of taste, there just is no other place
Like the N.O.R.T.H. P.O.L.E.

There's nowhere on the planet like the North Pole.
Bet you'll never want to leave.
It always smells of cakes, we don't make spelling
     mistakes
In the N.O.R.T.H. P.O.L.E.

Welcome to the North Pole, William.
Time to let the tour begin.
This is only our opinion,
But we think you're going to fit right in.

Welcome to the North Pole

'Welcome to the North Pole, children.
It's the land of make-believe.
There's no country greater, from Brazil down
    to Australia,
Than the N.O.R.T.H. P.O.L.E.!'

William, Brenda, Bob and Pamela whooped and cheered as the song ended and the elves took a bow. They saved the biggest applause for Starcloth, who held a long, deep bow until his assistants came rushing over with water and towels, which they dabbed on his sweaty brow as they ushered him away.

'That was **AMAZING**!' cried Brenda.

'Yes, it was. He really is a talented elf, that Starcloth,' Santa said, wiping a happy tear from his eye. 'Right, you've not come all this way just to watch elves dance and sing. This is a tour, after all. It will be inspirational!'

They all cheered again.

'Unexplainable!' He beamed.

They cheered louder!

'And educational . . .'

William and Brenda sighed.

'I just want to see the cool stuff William has been banging on about!' said Brenda.

'Brenda Payne, when it comes to *cool*, there's nowhere cooler than the North Pole: it is quite literally ice-cold!' Santa quipped as he began to lead his festive gang onward – but a low, sad roar stopped him in his tracks.

It was the Christmasaurus, standing beside William.

'Please, Santa, can the Christmasaurus come too?' William asked.

'Well, who am I to come between best friends? Of course he can come!' Santa agreed.

'Yes!' William cheered, and the Christmasaurus let out an excited chirp.

The Christmas gang was now complete and ready to explore!

CHAPTER FOUR

A FOREST FULL
OF WISHES

Have you ever made a wish?

Of course you have! Silly me.

OK, but have you ever *seen* a wish?

No, I didn't think so!

That's because the kind of wishes you can see only live in the forests surrounding the North Pole, and they only exist at Christmas.

Now I bet you're all thinking, *That's great, Mr Narrator, but what does a wish look like?*

Well, I'm glad you asked.

This is a wish:

'Ah, here they are,' whispered Santa as he gently pushed his way through the snow-covered Christmas trees and led Bob, Brenda, Pamela, William and the Christmasaurus towards some twinkling lights. 'These are wishes!'

As William got closer, he could see millions of sparkling, colourful creatures glowing in the trees.

A Forest Full of Wishes

'As you can see, they're small – about the size of a penny – with thin, barely visible wings. Listen closely and you'll hear them make a sort of twanging sound as they flap, like a ruler against a school desk,' Santa whispered.

'They're the most beautiful . . . things . . . I've ever . . . seen!' managed Bob, looking very overwhelmed.

'The most important part of a wish is the pointy antenna on the top of its head. This is its *wish-receptor*!' Santa explained.

'A *wish-re-what-er*?' Brenda asked.

'A *wish-receptor*! A wish's wish-receptor is a hyper-sensitive receiver of wishes tuned into the wish frequencies emitted by a person's brain. They're particularly attuned to the wish frequencies of children, though, and children make more wishes around Christmas than at any other time of year! Once they receive a wish signal, they are attracted to it like a moth to the moon and won't rest until it's granted.'

'Whoa! So that's why so many good things happen at Christmas?' William said.

'Precisely!' Santa smiled. 'You may also notice that wishes are covered in thick white fluff. This changes colour, depending on the kind of wish they will grant. Look, there's a chart on the tree,' he said, pointing at a piece of wood nailed to the nearest Christmas tree, which had a handy chart etched on to it. It said:

Blue = wishes for winning races

Green = wishes that are made on behalf of another person

Red = romantic wishes

Yellow = weather wishes

Orange = food wishes

Pink = health wishes

Gold = wealth wishes

Silver = simple wishes

Black = complicated wishes

Purple = mysterious wishes

'Of course, most wishes are multicoloured, because they're a combination of these things. For example, Bob, if you were to wish for sunshine so that you could win a race at William's school sports day, you'd need a wish with a dash of yellow for *weather* and a splodge of blue for *winning*, so you'd end up with a tinge of green too!' Santa explained.

Bob nodded eagerly, hanging on to Santa's every word. 'Not to be confused with an actual **green** wish that you make for another person, I suppose?' he added.

'Quite right! Jolly good, Mr Trundle. I'd better watch out or you'll be after my job!' Santa laughed, and Bob blushed happily while Pamela chuckled under her breath.

'We'll never hear the end of that!' she whispered to William and Brenda.

'What was that, my dear?' Santa asked.

'I said they're amazing – the wishes!' Pamela said, pointing at the shimmering white wishes in the trees. 'I wish I could hold one.'

All of a sudden, a glistening white ball of glowing fluff twanged through the air and flitted down towards her.

'Hold out your hand,' Santa instructed. 'Your wish is coming true.'

'My wish?' Pamela asked.

'Yes! You said *I wish I could hold one*, and so the wish is granting your wish,' Santa said, pointing to the small fluffball.

Pamela opened her palm and the wish landed softly

on it. Slowly, the white turned to bright silver.

'A simple wish!' said Santa, nodding happily.

'Are you seeing this?' Pamela squeaked as everyone huddled round her to get a closer look.

'It's so cute! Can we keep it?' Brenda asked.

'Oh, I'm afraid not, Brenda. Look . . .' Santa pointed at the wish as it started to fade.

'What's happening? Can't you stop it?' William asked – but it was too late. In just a few seconds, the wish wasn't there any more.

'Santa, where did it go?' William asked.

'Oh dear, I hope I didn't drop it!' Pamela muttered, searching in the snow around her feet.

'It's no use, my dear. That wish has fulfilled its purpose and has left us for good,' Santa explained.

'Left us? You mean it died?' Brenda whispered.

'Well, not exactly. You see, once a wish has come true, it's no longer needed any more, and so it fades away peacefully into nothing but stardust and dreams.'

'Like when a bumblebee uses its sting?' William asked.

'Yes, sort of, William. Both are precious, and not to be wasted! So you really must be careful what you wish for.' Santa then waved a hand at the glimmering trees. Three more small, white, fluffy wishes floated out of the branches and down towards Bob, Brenda and William.

'Now, as Pamela has had a wish, you can each take one home with you. But you must think carefully about how and when to use it.'

Instantly, the white wish hovering next to Bob turned a shimmering silver and began to glow intensely.

'Bob Trundle, have you made your wish already?' Santa chuckled.

'I couldn't help it!' said Bob, panicking.

Everyone gasped as a bright red Christmas jumper appeared in his hands. Flashing lights were knitted into the wool, and there was a large, shiny Christmas bauble in the centre. With shaking hands, Bob pressed the bauble, and 'Jingle Bells' began to play, the music echoing around the forest.

'**Whoa!**' the children gasped.

'More jumpers? Why is it always jumpers with you?' Pamela rolled her eyes with a smile.

'How did you do that?' Brenda asked.

'I just thought how much I'd love a new Christmas jumper. This is going to be my all-time favourite!' Bob said, excitedly slipping the jumper on. As he did so, the wish next to Brenda turned as black as ink.

'Ooooh, a complicated one!' Santa said. 'We don't see many of those!'

The wish spun round, its wings making a high-pitched twang as it started to glow brighter and brighter, until . . .

'It worked!' Brenda cheered, holding up a perfectly round snowball in her hands.

'A snowball?' William laughed. 'That doesn't seem very complicated. We're surrounded by snow! You could have just made one yourself. What a waste –

OUCH!'

The snowball donked William right on the nose, splatting snow across his face. It was a perfect shot. Then the tiny bits of snow started to rewind, reassembling themselves and turning back into the perfect snowball they'd formed before, and zooming through the air into Brenda's hand.

'I call it a Neverball. Never melts, never misses!' Brenda said, and poked her tongue out. 'I can't wait to take this to school with me. Oh, look – my wish!'

The little black wish had begun to fade. As they watched, it disappeared in the air in front of them, leaving just one white wish. William's.

The fluffy white creature flew down and landed gently in his lap.

'Hello!' William said with a smile.

The wish poked out a little hand and waved. William laughed.

The wish crawled around until it was tucked cosily inside William's warm pyjama pocket, lighting it up with its snowy white glow.

'Well, William, what's your wish?' Santa beamed excitedly.

William thought for a moment.

'I . . . I wish . . .' he stuttered as the glowing fluffy creature waited for its moment to shine, but it was no use. 'I can't do it! I can't make this creature fade into nothing. Look at it – it's too cute! You can come and live with me, little wish. I won't use you – I don't need anything,' William promised, gently patting his pocket.

'Very well! Bob has a new jumper, Brenda has a new snowball, and William has a new magical pet,' Santa said.

The Christmasaurus gave a sad little whimper.

'Oh, don't worry, Christmasaurus. You'll always be number one!' William said, placing a hand on the Christmasaurus's chilly nose. The wish popped out of his pocket and blew a cheeky raspberry at the dinosaur, before quickly hiding away again.

'Now then, we must continue the tour. There's still so much to see! Follow me!' Santa said, and he skipped onward through the forest full of wishes until they came out into a clearing on the other side. He spun round on the spot, beaming with excitement as he spread his arms wide and announced:

'Welcome to Elfville!'

CHAPTER FIVE
ELFVILLE

'Right this way – don't be shy!' Santa chuckled as he skipped into the first snowy street of Elfville. 'It's a tiny town of tiny houses that looks more like a town for tiny mouses . . . **Ha!** The elves must be rubbing off on me. Oh, and speaking of the elves – there they are!'

Waiting in an eager line to greet the visitors were Snozzletrump, Specklehump, Sparklefoot, Sugarsnout, Starlump, Snowcrumb, Spudcheeks and Sprout. Starlump was giddily bouncing up and down, while Snozzletrump was letting out excited bottom burps.

The Christmasaurus and the Winter Witch

'The elves couldn't wait for you to see where they live,' Santa whispered to William.

William stared around him. The miniature buildings were carved out of snow that was so tightly packed it was as solid as marble, with windows made of crystal-clear sheets of ice. And, even though it was tiny, it was a busy and bustling city, as grand as the streets of London.

'I visited a model village like this once. It even had a miniature river with boats that actually moved,' said Pamela.

'Well, this isn't a model village, Pam. May I call you Pam? It sounds like ham, and I do love a nice ham on Christmas Day. I know turkey is traditional, but . . . Sorry, I seem to have started talking about ham. Where was I? Ah yes! These tiny houses aren't toys or models. This is Elfville, North Pole . . . the number-one tourist destination for elfkind in the world!' Santa explained.

'Amazing!' Bob whispered, cleaning his glasses on his new Christmas jumper to get a clearer look.

Elves stared up at them or waved politely as they passed. Santa led the way through the crowded streets and William gazed at the shops selling all sorts of beautifully bizarre elf items. One had a window packed full of fluffy winter coats and a sign outside that read:

WINTER COATS STUFFED WITH 100 PER CENT MARSHMALLOW

'Actual marshmallows?' William asked Santa.

'Absolutely! What do you think keeps me so toasterifically warm in the sleigh on Christmas Eve? Plus, edible insulation can come in handy when you get a bit hot . . . or peckish,' Santa said with a wink, patting his thick red coat.

Next they passed a cosy-looking building. On the roof it had a hot tub full of mulled apple juice, in which three elves were relaxing. '*Snow spa*,' read William, looking at the sign outside.

'They do excellent pedicures,' Santa commented, 'although sadly I've never had one myself. My feet are too big to squidge through the front door.'

Further along the street, they passed:

* *a scented-candle shop that was in constant danger of melting from the heat of all the flames*
* *a snowball shop having a clearance sale*
* *a fresh crumpet bakery*
* *a clockmaker whose shop was ticking*
* *a clog cobbler whose shop was clopping*
* *a gizmologist whose window was full of gadgets made of brass and wood, magical instruments that William had never seen before.*

'This place is unbelievable!' said Brenda.

'**Shhhhh!**' hissed Santa, his finger pressed against his lips. 'Be careful with the *un*-word here.'

ELFVILLE

'What are those elves looking at?' Bob asked, pointing to a group of elves huddled together at a street corner, staring at something.

As the visitors got closer, they saw that the elves' faces were illuminated by the light of a tiny TV screen.

'What are the elves watching?' William asked.

'Let's go and look!' said Brenda, running over.

'I didn't fly you all the way to the North Pole to watch TV!' Santa said – but before he could usher them away the elves gasped at something on the screen.

Here's what they saw . . .

A busy street full of Christmas shoppers where one shop stood out from the rest. The sign above the entrance said MR P'S TOYSTORE in glowing green neon, and, as the doors opened, a cloud of dry ice poured out to reveal Mr P himself.

He was a tall man with a blinding white smile that radiated from his perma-tanned face. He wore a black pinstripe suit that was precisely tailored to his broad shoulders. The kind of suit William thought must have cost a lot of money, not like the baggy ones his dad wore to work.

Mr P's perfectly pressed shirt was buttoned up to his saggy neck skin and held in place with a thin black tie. He brushed his comb-over hairdo with his hands, taming the few wild strands, which were slicked down with enough oil to grease a Christmas turkey. On his chin he had the most suspicious of all facial-hair choices – a goatee!

'Oh no!' Pamela sighed.

'Who is that?' William asked.

'That's Mr P. You know, that guy who owns all those toyshops in town,' Brenda said quickly.

Suddenly the advert's jingle blasted out:

'*Who needs Santa any more?*
Waiting for Christmas is such a bore.
You can get anything you want and more,
RIGHT NOW, *at Mr P's Toystore!*'

Mr P skipped around one of his tacky toystores, chucking out presents from a big sack. The advert ended with these words written in bold across the screen, while being spoken by the same dramatic, deep-voiced guy who does all the action-movie trailers:

MR P'S TOYSTORE
WHEN SANTA'S NOT QUICK ENOUGH!

Silence fell over Elfville. William looked around, full of worry, but then there was an explosion of laughter. Starlump and Sprout were rolling around in the snow, holding their tummies, and even Santa let out a booming

'Ho ho!'

'Calm down, everyone, calm down,' he said, chuckling as he turned the TV off.

'"Who needs Santa any more?"' Bob gasped. 'The absolute cheek of it!'

'Oh, please!' Santa smiled. 'I've been upsetting toyshop owners for years by giving away toys! *It makes no business sense*, they tell me! They yell and shout and stomp their feet – but do they ever stop Christmas from coming?'

'NO!' cheered the elves.

'Not on your bowl full of jelly! It'll take more than TV advertising and a very, *very* expensive suit to keep me from leaping down chimneys,' Santa said confidently.

'But won't children be watching that? What if they decide not to wait until Christmas and just go and buy the toys they want with their pocket money?' William panicked. 'If they stop needing you, won't they stop believing in you?'

Santa paused. He looked at William, whose forehead was creased with worry. He reached into the inside pocket of his marshmallow-stuffed coat and pulled out something golden and shiny.

'What's that?' William asked.

'A thermometer?' Pamela guessed, looking at the delicate glass object.

'Of sorts, except this doesn't measure the temperature. It's a beliefometer,' Santa said, showing the magical device to William.

'What does it measure?' William asked.

'Jinglewatts,' Santa replied.

'*Jinglewatts?*' said William. 'What on earth is a jinglewatt?'

'My dearest William, it's how we measure belief!' Santa explained. 'And it's these jinglewatts that keep us in existence. We can get up to over a billion jinglewatts of belief during December!'

William leant in and saw a little red line that ran up a scale from **ZERO JINGLEWATTS** to **MAXIMUM JINGLEWATTS**.

'What happens if it hits zero?' William said.

'Well, as it's never happened, I'm not entirely sure, but my best guess is that all of us up at the North Pole would simply pop out of existence like we were never here to begin with,' Santa said.

'But you can't disappear! You're Santa!' William protested.

'Technically, I'm afraid I *could* disappear, William. Without a single jinglewatt of belief to keep Christmas alive, I'd just fade away into nothing, like a snowman in the sun or a pop star in their thirties.'

'What about the Christmasaurus?' William asked. 'Would he disappear too?'

'Oh no, he's fine, William. You give him all the belief he needs to shine as brightly as the winter moon,' Santa said, smiling, and the Christmasaurus gave William a slightly embarrassed nudge of thanks.

'Plus, I have something here at the North Pole that Mr P could never have. Something better than all the Christmas puddings in the world piled on to one giant plate, dripping with dollops of double cream, with wafts of sweet warm steam filling the – Hang on a tick, what was I saying? Ah yes, the *thing*! It's very old and very magical . . . William, you may remember it!'

A smile spread over William's face as he realized what Santa was describing.

'Shall we show them, William?' Santa asked, beaming.

ELFVILLE

'Ooh yes, yes, yes! I mean, yes please, Santa,' Bob answered, a little flustered.

Santa turned to two of the elves. 'Snowcrumb, Spudcheeks, meet us in the Snow Ranch,' he told them. They nodded and raced away like excited schoolchildren trying to be the first one there.

'Now follow me!' Santa cried, and he led them over a bridge out of Elfville. They crossed a flowing river of warm mince-pie filling, went through a candy cave with red-and-white walls where candy canes hung like icicles from the ceiling, past the library of Christmas stories and the cinema showing only Christmas movies – until they finally stopped at the top of a long toboggan run.

'Right then, who's first?' Santa said with a smile as he pulled several rickety wooden toboggans from a rack at the edge of the drop.

They looked down at the steep, icy slope.

'You must be kidding – it's a vertical drop!' cried Pamela.

'Is that a loop-the-loop?' Bob asked.

'Indeed it is!' replied Santa.

'Awesome!' William said, and the Christmasaurus roared in agreement.

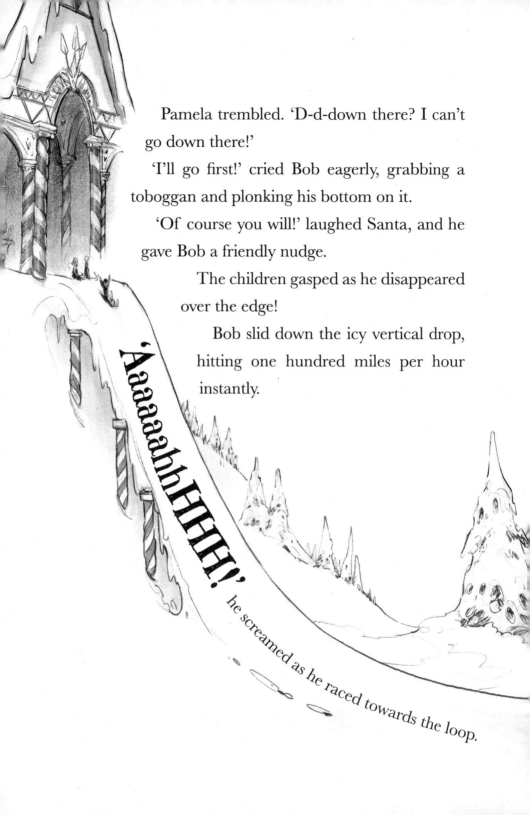

Pamela trembled. 'D-d-down there? I can't go down there!'

'I'll go first!' cried Bob eagerly, grabbing a toboggan and plonking his bottom on it.

'Of course you will!' laughed Santa, and he gave Bob a friendly nudge.

The children gasped as he disappeared over the edge!

Bob slid down the icy vertical drop, hitting one hundred miles per hour instantly.

'AaaaaahhHHH!' he screamed as he raced towards the loop.

'He's never going to make it!' Pamela
yelled.

But he did!

'YAHOO!!!'

Bob cried with joy as he whirled round
the loop-the-loop. He slid to a stop at
the bottom – and stared.

He was right outside Santa's Snow Ranch!

'This is where Santa lives . . .?' he called, his voice trembling at the sight of the grandest log cabin in existence. It was made of pine trees from the northern forest, making it as tall as a giant and wider than fourteen frosty football pitches.

'Me next!' Brenda leapt on to a toboggan and plunged down the run, screaming and whooping with joy. William watched her disappear over the edge, loop the loop and slide right up next to his dad.

'Come on, Mum – it's fine!' Brenda called up.

'OK, my dear . . . Coming!' Pamela edged towards the drop. The sight made her knees so wobbly that she fell head first down the slope, barely clinging on to her toboggan.

'Head first? Show-off!' Brenda shouted, laughing as her mum joined her and Bob.

It was Santa's turn next, and he whipped out an expandable red toboggan that had been hidden somewhere in his coat pocket. It unfolded itself in less

than a second into a miniature version of his sleigh. Santa performed a backward somersault into the drop, giving William a salute as he landed on the mini sleigh.

William carefully went to the edge and looked down nervously.

'Pretty high!' he said as the Christmasaurus stepped up next to him. 'Shall we go together?' he suggested.

The Christmasaurus nodded and a cheeky grin crept over his scaly face.

'OK then. I don't need one of those,' he said as the Christmasaurus began pulling a crooked old sledge from the rack. 'Who needs a toboggan when you've got a wheelchair?' He grinned as he lined up the wheels of his chair. 'Ready? One . . . two –'

But, before William reached *three*, his dinosaur friend gave him a little push with his scaly tail, sending him over the edge first!

'ThreeeeEEEEEEEE!'

William screamed as he plummeted down the slope, the wheels of his chair spinning desperately.

The Christmasaurus shot down after him, his shiny feet tucked underneath him.

'That's cheating – you're flying!' William screamed as the dinosaur flew behind him, nudging him with his nose to give William a speed-boost round the loop-the-loop.

To Bob, Pamela and Brenda, watching from the bottom of the run, William and the Christmasaurus were just a blurry flash of blue as they zoomed round the winding toboggan run.

'Can we do it again?' Brenda pleaded.

'Ho-no, not now! We have so much else to see!' Santa said, stepping up to the enormous wooden doors of his Snow Ranch. 'Let's go!'

Santa led them all through smaller, more sensibly sized doors that were cut into the ridiculously large doors and they entered the grandest entrance hall you could possibly imagine . . .

You want to try? Go ahead!

Imagine **gigantic**, quadruple-height ceilings . . . Keep going . . . a little taller than that.

Whoa! Stop!

That's just silly! Bring them down a tad . . . There! That looks about right.

The floors are made of huge slabs of Christmas-tree pine that are as warm as a cup of tea under your feet. That's because the underfloor-heating system uses actual English breakfast tea to heat the pipes.

The air smells of fresh *vaninnamon*, and the sounds of

carols and pointless family bickering – the true sounds of Christmas – echo from somewhere in the distance.

The visitors couldn't believe their eyes, ears or noses.

'Come in, come in! Welcome to my home.' Santa grinned as he spun round merrily with his arms wide.

'This place is amazing!' Brenda gawped.

'We have everything you could possibly imagine, and a few things you probably can't,' Santa said with a chuckle.

Two elves suddenly appeared in the entrance hall as though they had been there the entire time.

'Your Merriness, sir?' they said.

'Spudcheeks, Snowcrumb, how can I help you?' Santa asked.

'The crumpets are toasted and ready for tasting! The turkey is roasted and ready for basting!'

chimed Spudcheeks and Snowcrumb in perfect unison.

Santa smiled excitedly. 'Very good! But first we're going to see *the tree.*'

CHAPTER SIX
THE OLDEST CHRISTMAS TREE

'Follow me! Follow me!' Santa sang as he skipped down the wooden hallway of his supersized log cabin, its walls decorated with colourful drawings from children around the world.

He did a little cartwheel and went into a forward roll, then pushed open heavy double doors to what looked like a library.

'Books?' Brenda scoffed.

'These aren't books – these are the lists,' Santa said, running his fingers over the ancient spines of thick tomes that lined every wall.

'You mean, **the** Nice List?' Bob asked.

'And the Naughty one,' Santa replied, pointing to the opposite wall, which housed an equally daunting number of books.

'Let's find Brenda's name in there!' William teased.

'Hey!' She nudged him. 'That was the old me!'

'Oh, I think it would take you forever to find her name anyway, William. There are just so many of them. Every child, good and bad, naughty and nice, to whom I've ever delivered presents is in these lists.' Santa smiled. 'But that's not what I want to show you.'

William, Brenda, Bob, Pamela and the Christmasaurus followed Santa to the back of the room where a grand writing desk took up almost the entire width of the wall. Sitting on top of the desk was a very old, very crooked, very magical Christmas tree.

'This was the first Christmas tree ever to exist . . . *EVER!*' Santa said with wonder in his voice.

'Now that's better than books!' said Brenda.

'LISTS!' William reminded her.

'Shhh! I want to know about the tree! What are those things hanging on it?' Brenda asked, pointing to the peculiar pods that were sprouting from among the pine needles.

'*Bean pods!*' William said in excitement.

'Correct, William! Let me show you how it works, Brenda.'

Santa shot round his desk and plopped his bottom on to a huge rocking chair.

From a large pile he picked up a piece of paper that had a crayon drawing of himself. He cleared his throat and began to read aloud – not to William, Brenda, Bob, Pamela or the Christmasaurus. He was reading to the tree!

'*Dear Santa, for Christmas, please could I have a brand-new telescope to see the stars? Merry Christmas, Phoebe Goosens.*'

Then everything went quiet. Santa held his finger to his lips and they all waited and watched.

POP!

'What was that?' asked Brenda, startled.

'And what's that on the tree?' cried Pamela.

'It's the pod containing the bean that will eventually grow into young Phoebe's telescope,' Santa said, grinning from ear to ear.

'Grow?' said Brenda. 'I thought the elves made all the presents?'

'Well, you obviously didn't read the first book!' Santa said. 'Now then, I have a very special gift for you, William and Brenda.'

THE OLDEST CHRISTMAS TREE

'YES! I **love** presents!' Brenda said excitedly, rubbing her hands together. 'It's not a book, though, right?'

'Oh, I hope it is!' said William, smiling. 'A dinosaur one!'

The Christmasaurus roared in agreement.

'It might very well be that,' said Santa. 'You see, it's the gift of whatever you want!'

William and Brenda looked at each other, confused.

'Whatever we want?' said William.

'Yes, absolutely anything! I thought that since you're here at the North Pole this year, rather than you both writing me letters and wasting money on stamps and envelopes, I would give you both a raw bean!' Santa said mysteriously.

'Ew!' said Brenda, her nostrils flaring.

'No, no!' Santa laughed. 'A raw bean is a bean with no present assigned to it. A blank canvas, so to speak! Once you know what you want, all you need to do is whisper it, very clearly and precisely, to your bean.'

'And then what?' Bob blurted out, hardly able to contain himself at the thought of these mysterious, magical beans.

'Then you simply plant it in a snowfield and . . .'
Santa paused, realizing the problem with his plan. 'Ah,
you don't have a snowfield, do you?'

William and Brenda shook their heads.

'Ice mine?' Santa said hopefully.

Even more head-shaking.

'It's often wet and muddy over Christmas, and it's
not usually cold enough for the snow to stay,' Pamela
pointed out.

'Right . . . that won't do at all! The beans need to be
planted somewhere below freezing. It's what activates
the magic, you see!' Santa said, scratching his beard.

'What about putting them in the freezer?' William
suggested.

'Bingo!' cried Santa. 'Why didn't I think of that?
It's like a snowfield in a box! Absolutely brilliant idea,
William. Smart boy – always knew you were! Just clear
a little space in your freezer next to the fish fingers, and
whack your bean in there! Genius. That should work
nicely!'

Santa turned to the tree and leant in close.

'Right then, tree – it's Santa here, and I've got

a special request. I'll have a raw bean for William, please – one that's good and ready to grow into something marvellous, I've no doubt!'

The tree suddenly hunched over, almost as though it were laying an egg, and . . . **POP!**

Something green and as large as a pine cone had appeared on one of the lower branches.

It was a bean pod!

'Well, jingle me sideways, that's a plump one! You'll get something terrific out of that, William!' Santa boomed.

William went closer to the tree and plucked the pod from the branch.

'Thank you, tree, almost done. We'll have one more raw bean just like that for Brenda here, please,' Santa requested.

'This is SO good! OMG, I've got SOOOO many things I want to ask it for,' Brenda said at a million miles per second.

'Well, make sure it's something good, and don't waste it! It'll only grow **one** present!' Santa said.

'Just one?' Brenda whined.

'Just one!' Santa confirmed.

The tree shuddered, shaking off some of its ancient pine needles.

'Brenda who? Brenda *Payne*!' Santa answered.

'Is he having a conversation with the tree?' Brenda whispered to William.

'I think so,' he replied in astonishment.

'OK . . . Just making sure I wasn't imagining it,' Brenda said.

'I told you trees talk,' Bob whispered to William.

'How odd,' Santa said, searching in the tree for the bean.

'What is it?' William asked.

'Well, I've never known it not to dish out a bean pod before. Tree, did you hear me? Quick as a tick now – we haven't got all day. I'm very sorry about this, everyone. Trees are stubborn things, you know,' Santa said, giving the tree's roots a little tap.

The tree responded. It wobbled a bit, making Brenda jump back.

Then it shook itself again, causing more of its pine

needles to fall to the floor. Next the tree looked as though it was straining, as if it was trying its hardest not to let this raw bean pod pop out!

'What's going on?' asked Brenda, frowning. 'Where's my magic bean?'

'By jingle, I don't know,' muttered Santa. 'This is most strange. The tree seems to have decided – well . . .'

'WHAT?' demanded Brenda.

'Well, it seems to have decided not to sprout a bean pod for you,' Santa explained, a little uncomfortably. 'I, er . . . well, it suspects you would do something rather naughty with it.'

'But I'm **NICE** now!' shouted Brenda, stamping her foot so hard that the tree gave another little wobble, so that it shed a few more of its needles – though there weren't many to begin with! 'I'm on the **NICE LIST!** You said so yourself!'

'Oh dear, what a pickle. Don't worry though, Brenda – you can still send me your Christmas letter, just like any other year!'

'A letter? **A LETTER?** Willypoos gets a magical Christmas bean that's going to grow into

99

whatever he wants, and I have to write you a stinking letter?' wailed Brenda.

'That does seem a little unfair,' said Pamela, looking at Bob.

'Oh, come on now – it's thanks to William that we're all here, having this wonderful day!' Bob pointed out. 'Let him enjoy his magic bean, eh, Brenda?'

'Well, that's just typical, isn't it? Perfect little Willypoos getting all the good stuff while I have to sit and watch,' Brenda mumbled to herself. 'I might as well be back on the Naughty List.'

'What was that? Didn't quite catch the end,' Santa said, cleaning out his ear with his finger.

'I said, *fine*! I'll write you a letter like everyone else. Enjoy your bean, Willypoos,' Brenda said – although, judging by the way she said it, William could tell she didn't really want him to enjoy it.

'Wonderful. That's what Christmas is all about!' said Santa happily, and clapped his hands. The doors suddenly flew open, and Snozzletrump, Specklehump, Sparklefoot, Sugarsnout, Starlump, Spudcheeks, Snowcrumb and Sprout waddled into the room, carrying a camping stove and a large cooking pot.

The elves plonked these down on the floor in front of William, and Sugarsnout filled the pot with water.

'Thank you, elves. Now, William, pop your bean pod into the water,' Santa instructed.

William did as he was told, and watched as the water began to bubble.

'Keep a close eye on it . . .' Santa said.

'It's doing something!' said William.

'Good, good! Elves?' Santa summoned his helpers.

Starlump twirled over to the pot, peeped inside and gave Santa the thumbs up. Santa then pulled a spoon from the inside pocket of his red coat, dipped it in the water and scooped out a large white bean with red swirls that was about the size of a hard-boiled egg.

'What's that?' Pamela asked.

Santa grinned. 'This is what's inside each bean pod. The magic bean itself! It's the part that you speak to, the part you need to plant in the freezer . . . the part from which William's present will grow! Righty-ho, William, I've written down clear instructions on how to properly care for your bean. Be sure to follow them very carefully and you'll have whatever you wish for in your snowfield . . . sorry, freezer . . . by Christmas!'

Sprout handed William a little card, which William tucked into his pyjama pocket. He was careful not to squash his wish, which gave a friendly little squeak and wiggled to one side to make room.

Suddenly Santa's eyes lit up and he snapped his fingers. 'All this talk of freezers has given me an idea! How would you all like to visit the North Pole kitchen?'

'Is there nice food?' Brenda said hopefully.

'Nice food? Why, this is the North Pole! Tell them, elves,' Santa said, and the elves started singing as they marched the family out of the door to the kitchen:

> 'We've got candy canes,
> Crumpets,
> Mince pies
> And crumpets,
> Gingerbread,
> Fruit cake
> And did we mention crumpets?

The Oldest Christmas Tree

Nut roast,
Cookie dough.
Now open wide
For a big roast turkey
With crumpets stuffed inside.

We hardly throw a scrap away,
It tastes too good to dump it.
And the greatest taste in all the land
Is yes, you guessed it,
CRUMPETS!

Crumpets, crumpets, crumpets, hey!
Yum-diddly-nom-nom-diddly.
Crumpets, crumpets, crumpets, hey!
Yum-diddly-nom-nom-diddly!

Crumpets make our tongues scream YES!
Our tummies go all fluttery.
Toasted crumpets are the best,
When they're nice and buttery!

Oh!

Crumpets, crumpets, crumpets, hey!
Yum-diddly-nom-nom-diddly.
Crumpets, crumpets, crumpets, hey!
Yum-diddly-nom-nom-diddly!

Breakfast, brunch, lunch, dinner or snack,
Crumpets all day long.
We love crumpets so much that
We wrote this crumpet song.

Oh!

Crumpets, crumpets, crumpets, hey!
Yum-diddly-nom-nom-diddly.
Crumpets, crumpets, crumpets, hey!
Yum-diddly-nom-nom-diddly!'

When they finally made it to the kitchen (after twenty-six more choruses of the crumpet song), it was beautifully busy with elves, all working with purpose and determination, and William saw that, luckily, Brenda seemed to have cheered right up.

It was all '*Yes, Chef!*' this and '*No, Chef!*' that as they skipped and danced round the ovens. Brews and stews of all colours and smells bubbled and boiled on the hot stoves while the tiny elves worked in teams to stir and taste their culinary creations.

Starlump handed out bite-sized bits of fresh crumpet, while Spudcheeks poured them each a goblet of ice-cold milk. But it was when Spudcheeks opened the fridge to put the milk back that William noticed something strange.

Spudcheeks didn't just place the milk in the fridge. No, the elf stepped *inside* the refrigerator, disappearing completely as the door closed behind him!

William couldn't believe his eyes.

'What the . . .?' he whispered.

'Did you just see what I just saw?' Brenda asked, her eyes on the fridge too.

'More crumpets, children?' Starlump interrupted quickly.

'Not on your nelly,' said William as he wheeled himself over to the fridge.

105

'What is it, Willypoos?' Bob asked, noticing William's puzzled expression and stepping over to join him. Pamela and Brenda followed close behind, not wanting to miss out on whatever magic had made the elf disappear into the fridge.

Santa suddenly realized what they were up to.

'Oh, I wouldn't open that if I were –'

He didn't get to finish that sentence before William had gripped the door handle and pulled the fridge door open.

'It's just an ordinary fridge!' William said with a frown.

And it was. There were a few shelves with some veg, cartons of milk, eggs and that was all.

'But where's Smudgechops?' asked Brenda.

'It's *Spudcheeks*!' came a voice.

'Did that just come from the *freezer*?' asked Pamela, pointing to the lower door.

'Children, I really don't think we've got time to –'

But, before Santa could finish that second warning, Brenda had opened the freezer door.

THE OLDEST CHRISTMAS TREE

There was a rush of ice-cold air and, with a

SWOOSh, William, Brenda, Bob and Pamela vanished!

CHAPTER SEVEN
SUB-ZERO

'Ow! Get your foot off my face!' snapped Brenda.

'Get your face off my foot!' replied William.

'What happened?' asked Bob.

'Where are we?' said Pamela.

'Wherever we are, it's **FREEZING**!' William said, shivering through chattering teeth.

They were gathered together in the middle of what could only be described as a huge white box. There were frosty white walls and a frosty white ceiling, and the whole room was lit by a single light at the back that made everyone look as pale as polar bears.

'Er . . . Bob, I think you should see this . . .' muttered Pamela, who was facing the opposite way to everyone else.

Bob, William and Brenda spun round – and what they saw blew their minds.

'Is that a giant packet of fish fingers?' said Brenda, staring up at the enormous cardboard box that towered over their heads.

'And those potato waffles are bigger than our house!' said William.

'I don't think they are big . . . I think we are small!' Bob said.

'Yes, you are! Smaller than a pimple on a flea's bum,' Santa said, his voice exploding from overhead so loudly that they all had to cover their ears. 'Oh, sorry, is this better?' he whispered.

'Yes!' William said.

'Sorry, was that a yes? You'll have to speak up!' Santa said.

'**YES!**' the tiny freezer gang screamed.

Santa was staring down at them, his face as big as an

IMAX cinema screen. The Christmasaurus appeared behind Santa, peering in excitedly, and a dollop of dino slobber dropped from his wagging tongue. Brenda leapt out of the way as the enormous glob of slob splashed down next to her, freezing as it touched the icy floor.

'Oi, watch it!' she yelled up to the gigantic Christmasaurus, who closed his mouth sheepishly.

'Where are we?' William called.

'You're in the freezer!' Santa said, as though it were quite normal to be sucked into a freezer and shrunk down to the size of a pea!

All of a sudden, there was a rustling sound from behind one of the boxes of frozen chips.

SUB-ZERO

'Did anyone else hear that?' asked Pamela with a nervous tremble in her voice.

'No, no, it's nothing! Everyone just climb on to my hand and we'll continue the tour . . .' Santa said, placing his jumbo hand in the freezer with an open palm ready for the family to climb on to.

But then they heard it again, that same rustling sound, as though someone or something was inside the freezer with them.

'I don't think we're alone in here,' said William, backing away from the frozen food.

'That's it, William – move on to my hand. Come on now, all of you,' Santa pleaded – and William thought he could hear a note of panic in Santa's usually jolly voice.

But, before he had a chance to ask why, a small head popped out of a packet of frozen raspberries. It belonged to a funny-looking creature with long, sticky-up ears.

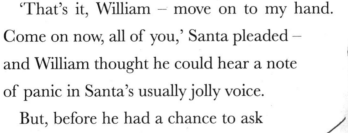

Perched on these sticky-up ears was a baby-blue flat cap, and on the creature's nose was a pair of thick glasses with ice cubes for lenses.

'Oo's there?' the creature said in a croaky voice as it looked around.

'I'm William Trundle and this is my family. We're with Santa . . . on a tour . . .' William said nervously. 'It's a pleasure to meet you . . .'

'Zero,' the creature barked. 'Sub-Zero.' And with that he tipped his hat and dived back into the packet of frozen raspberries.

'Right, jump on now before he comes back!' Santa whispered from above.

'Is that Santa I hear?' Sub-Zero snapped from somewhere inside the packet of fruit.

'Hello, Sub . . .' Santa sighed, and leapt into the freezer himself, instantly shrinking down to the same size as the children.

'Got me working double overtime. Makes no sense, no sense at all. It's not Christmas for over a week yet and I'm in 'ere, freezing my fingers off . . .' Sub-Zero muttered to himself.

SUB-ZERO

William watched as he dragged out a huge tub of lemon sorbet. He then gave the enormous box of potato waffles a whopping kick with his pointy foot, causing a huge frozen waffle to fall out of the box next to the sorbet tub. Using the waffle as a ladder, Sub-Zero climbed up, popped the lid off the sorbet and shoved a thermometer into the delicious-looking dessert.

The temperature reading plummeted instantly, and Sub-Zero gave a satisfied little nod before reaching into the pocket of his lab coat and pulling out a keyring with a selection of silver spoons. He chose the smallest spoon, scooped up a teeny bit of sorbet and popped it on to his pale blue tongue.

After a second, he grabbed his head and winced in agony.

'Is he OK?' William asked, feeling worried about the funny little creature. He looked as though he had a terrible headache.

'Oh yes, he's quite all right,' Santa said as they all watched.

'What's he doing?' Pamela asked.

'Testing it,' Santa replied.

'For what?' asked William.

'Brain-freezeability!' Santa said. 'How is it, Sub?'

'This one's got quite a kick to it!' Sub-Zero said, breaking through the brain freeze.

The strange little creature then opened up his coat, revealing row upon row of pockets that held hundreds of tiny glass vials with cork stoppers. He slid one out, removed the cork with his teeth and filled it with the freezing-cold sorbet. While his lab coat was hanging open, William saw that each glass vial inside was filled with all sorts of wonderfully cold sorbets and ice creams, some of them glowing and swirling like magic potions.

Sub-Zero replaced the stopper, slipped the lemon

sorbet into a pocket and buttoned his lab coat back up.

'Santa, is he an elf?' William asked as the creature slid down the waffle ladder.

Sub-Zero froze, but one of his pointed ears twitched in William's direction.

'An elf?' he said, turning slowly to face William while rolling up the sleeves of his lab coat, as though ready to thump someone on the nose. 'Did somebody just call me a ruddy *elf*?'

'No, no, no, Sub-Zero. Nobody called you an elf!' Santa said soothingly.

'Good. Cos I ain't no blinkin' singin', dancin', rhymin' elf. I'm a snow sprite,' he said, sticking his pointy little nose in the air with pride.

'Sprite? I thought that was a fizzy drink!' laughed Brenda. She didn't know that you should never, ever laugh at a sprite.

WHACK!

A ball of freezer frost splat-biffed Brenda right on the nose!

'Nobody laughs at a sprite,' Sub-Zero croaked. 'Am I funny now?'

'No, no!' winced Brenda, a little stunned at being on the receiving end of a snowball for once.

'Good. Let that be a lesson. A sprite is a sprite. Not an elf, not a fizzy drink,' huffed Sub-Zero.

'He's a grumpy little thing, isn't he?' William whispered to Santa.

'Yes, his great-grandfather was a Creaker,' Santa explained.

'Now, if you don't mind, I've got to mix this potion together or time will be catching up with you,' Sub-Zero snapped.

'Time? Catching up with *us*?' Bob said, sounding interested.

'Of course, you silly little human,' snapped the sprite.

'My goodness, how do you think everyone back in your town is frozen in time while you're here? It doesn't happen by itself, does it!'

'I think we've heard enough now,' said Santa with a nervous giggle. 'Let's get back to the –'

'You've not told 'em 'bout *her* . . . have you, Santa?' Sub-Zero said, a mischievous grin spreading across his face.

'Told us about who?' asked Brenda.

'No one! Now who wants to see the stables?' Santa said, trying to usher the children away from the sprite.

'Stables? Reindeer?' scoffed the sprite. 'Who wants to see them when you could see the –'

'Don't!' Santa interrupted.

'When you could see the –' teased Sub-Zero.

'I mean it, Sub!' Santa warned.

The little creature looked ready to burst with naughtiness. 'OK, I won't tell them anything,' he said.

Santa let out a relieved sigh.

Sub-Zero grinned wickedly. 'Especially anything about the **Winter Witch.**'

CHAPTER EIGHT
THE WINTER WITCH

All the little hairs on William's neck stood on end as though some sort of magic were floating through the air. Or maybe he was just cold. Perhaps a bit of both!

'The Winter **WHAT?!**' Pamela shrieked.

'Witch!' said Sub-Zero, making his gruff voice sound even spookier than it already was.

'Calm down, calm down. There's no need to worry. She's not that sort of witch,' said Santa.

'But witches aren't meant to be around at this time of year. Halloween is for witches, not Christmas. Autumn,

118

not winter!' Bob said, trying to understand this new piece of Christmas information.

'Ah, but not the *Winter* Witch. She's always around. Now, then, today, yesterday, tomorrow . . .' Sub-Zero said mysteriously. From the cheeky grin on his face, and the troubled expression on Santa's, William saw that the sprite knew full well that Santa had been trying to keep this quiet.

'What's he on about, Santa?' asked Brenda.

Santa sighed. 'All right. I'll tell you if I must, but this is not to be repeated,' he said very seriously.

The family all looked at each other excitedly. Everyone loves a secret!

'The North Pole, as you know, is home to many magical creatures: elves, flying reindeer . . .'

'A dinosaur!' added William.

'Yes, and a dinosaur,' Santa said with a smile.

Sub-Zero coughed meaningfully.

'*And* sprites, although I'm not sure for how much longer,' Santa added, glaring crossly at Sub-Zero. 'But there's one person who nobody knows about, who no one has ever known about.'

He gazed at them for a moment.

'She's the best-kept Christmas secret of all,' Santa whispered, 'which is surprising, because she is so powerful that Christmas itself would not exist without her. She's older than time itself, yet still as young as tomorrow. She is known only as the Winter Witch.'

William felt that same shivery, icy tingle every time he heard this mysterious name.

Brenda blinked. '*Older than time itself, yet still as young as tomorrow?* That makes absolutely no sense to me.'

'Think of it like this. Time is like a snowflake . . .' Santa said as he plucked a large flake of frost from the white walls of the fridge and held it up to the light for everyone to see. It was as big as a dinner plate, even in Santa's chunky hands, which allowed everyone to see all the intricate lines stretching out like an icy spider's web.

'You see, it has many beautiful frozen branches – what I like to call frosticles – spiralling out from the centre in every thinkable direction. In the same way, today won't just flow into tomorrow in one simple, straight line – no, there are many possible paths for us to take into the future. The paths we choose dictate the shape of the snowflake of our lives,' Santa said.

'I think I get it,' said Brenda. 'Wait . . . no, I don't get it at all, actually. Can you say all that again, but better?'

Santa scratched his beard. 'This is tricky. I've never had to explain magical time travel before!' he admitted. 'Let's imagine you woke up and decided to put on your favourite pair of shoes. You go for a walk feeling splendiferous and happy, and so the frosticle of your day is born. Each step in your comfy shoes takes you further down this particular branch.

'However, let's start that day again, but instead of your comfy shoes you put on a brand-new pair of boots that haven't been worn in yet. They're a bit tight, but you decide to stick with them. A different-shaped frosticle has started, only this one is a bit sharper, more jagged, and each step you take in these boots that rub is another moment of time added to your snowflake.'

Brenda waved her hand in the air with a question.

'Yes, Brenda?' Santa asked.

'Can't you just change which frosti . . . frostica . . .'

'Frosticle?'

'Yeah, that! Can't you just jump from the bad one to the good one?' Brenda suggested.

'Well done, young Brenda, that's a grand idea. Wouldn't it be wonderful if you could just make a bad decision, then leap over to a different timeline – a different frosticle of your snowflake – in which you had never made that bad decision?'

They all nodded.

'Well, I'm afraid there is only one person alive who has ever done that,' Santa said.

'Let me guess. The Winter Witch?' said William.

'Correctamundo!'

Santa boomed. '*That* is what made her . . . well, the way she is today. She's the only one powerful enough to freeze time and explore all its possibilities. How else do you think I travel round the world on Christmas Eve in just one night? With the help of the Winter Witch! She freezes time, and allows me to slip through it and get my job done. Why, she's the one keeping today on pause for us!'

'So why are we not frozen, like all the people back home?' Brenda asked.

'Because I asked her not to freeze you, unlike the rest of the world. She is a masterful manipulator of time, Brenda, and once it's frozen she can bend it to her will,' explained Santa. 'The Winter Witch can leave certain people unfrozen – and, in fact, every Christmas Eve I choose just a few children around the world to remain unfrozen, so that they hear the jingle of sleigh bells as I fly overhead. It helps to keep the magic of Christmas alive! So, if you ever wake up during the night on Christmas Eve, you know you're one of the lucky few.'

'That happened to us last Christmas, Brenda!' William realized.

'**Whoa!**' Brenda whispered.

'But where did she come from?' William asked Santa.

'That's the biggest mystery of all, William,' he replied. But William could have sworn he saw a strange expression pass across Santa's face as he said it.

'So how exactly does the Winter Witch freeze time?' Brenda asked.

'Oh, that one's easy. By brain freeze!' Santa said with a grin.

'You mean, like when you drink a milkshake too fast?' said William.

'Yep!'

'Or swallow an entire scoop of ice cream in one gulp?' said Bob.

'Exactly!' said Santa with a smile.

'So why can't we all freeze time?' asked Brenda.

'That's where I come in!' Sub-Zero gave a bow. 'The Winter Witch doesn't just get any old brain freeze. It's a special Sub-Zero-induced brain freeze. I'm her personal magical mixologist.' He proudly

flashed the vials of frozen slush inside his lab coat. 'Want to see me mix?'

'**YES!**' they all cheered excitedly in unison, sounding almost like elves themselves.

Sub-Zero quickly shoved and heaved the enormous boxes and packets of frozen food aside, which was quite an achievement for such a tiny little creature. When everything was moved, the sprite uncovered in the back corner of the freezer what seemed to be a large glass bowl suspended over a pile of ice.

'What's that?' William asked.

'It's my *cold*ron,' explained Sub-Zero. 'It's the only container able to hold liquid at temperatures well below freezing.' He whipped out two vials. 'A dash of lemon sorbet, a splodge of raspberry ripple and, finally, the secret ingredient that makes it colder than any other liquid in the world . . .'

William's eyes lit up at the sound of this mysterious ingredient.

'A few shavings of North Pole ice,' Sub-Zero said, throwing a few shards of blue ice into the coldron.

Then he held his hand out underneath the glass bowl and snapped his pointy little fingers.

There was a sudden **flash** that made everyone jump.

'Look, the fire is blue!' cried William, pointing at the flickering azure flame underneath the coldron.

'That's not fire, you little twerp. It's erif!' snapped Sub-Zero.

'Erif? What's erif?' asked Brenda.

'You lot are slower than a squished snail,' hissed the unfriendly sprite.

Then it clicked in William's head. 'It's *fire* backwards. Erif – fire. See?'

'Oh yeah!' said Brenda. 'Cool!'

'It's colder than cool! And erif isn't fire backwards. Fire is erif backwards. You lot just get it all muddled up, as usual,' said Sub-Zero grumpily. 'Now hush a moment. I need to concentrate on this bit.'

He pulled out his keyring of spoons, selected the longest one and dipped it in. The supercooled liquid was bubbling and frothing as he started to swirl it together.

'Nobody makes a brain-freeze potion like a North Pole sprite,' Santa whispered as they watched Sub-Zero

check the temperature.

'It's ready!' he announced, grinning.

The sprite quickly pulled out a whistle from underneath his lab coat and gave an almighty blow. The sound was deafening in the confined freezer drawer. The ground shook alarmingly beneath their feet and the light switched off, plunging them into darkness.

'What's going on?' Pamela screamed.

'Collection time!' Sub-Zero said.

At that, William saw a gigantic, gloved elf hand reach down and pluck up the coldron of freezing liquid, which looked just like one of the sprite's vials in its massive fingers. It closed the drawer again and the freezer light popped back on.

'Where are they taking it?' William asked.

'It goes straight to Her Witchfulness,' Sub-Zero said proudly.

'Can we see her?' Brenda asked Santa.

William thought Santa's face looked pale, all of a sudden. 'Absolutely not,' Santa said. 'She's in a secret, hidden place. It is forbidden.'

'Please!' Brenda pleaded.

Santa shook his head. 'Nope! Totally forbidden.'

'PLEEEEAAAASE!'

'Not a chance!' he insisted.

'Won't you even tell us where she is?' Brenda said.

Sub-Zero let out a little chuckle to himself as he packed away his tools.

'He already *told* you where she is,' the sprite said, laughing. 'Well, nice meeting you all. Enjoy your time here. Stay away from the *forbidden*.'

He winked as he spun on the spot, wrapping his lab coat around his tiny body like a cloak, before vanishing into thin air.

'What did he mean, *you already told us*?' asked Brenda, frowning.

Santa pretended not to have heard the question. 'Right, what do you say we get out of here and find somewhere less chilly?' he replied quickly, clapping his

hands. 'This way, one at a time, down here.'
He pointed to a small slope that led through a
hole in the freezer wall back into the kitchen.

'What's that?' Pamela asked. 'Not another
toboggan run?'

'Ice dispenser! Off you go!' Santa said,
nodding down the chute.

William wanted to be first this time. He
shot straight over and wheeled himself down
the slide without stopping.

'WheeeeEEEEEE!'

he cried as he slid down the ice dispenser,
out of the freezer, and popped into the
North Pole kitchen, instantly returning to
his normal size.

The Christmasaurus, who had been
waiting patiently by the freezer, greeted
him with a giant lick across the face.

'Would you stop that!' William giggled.
'Let's help the others out. Can you get
me a glass from up there?' He pointed

to a high kitchen cupboard full of glasses that was just out of his reach.

The Christmasaurus leapt at the chance to help. He stretched his neck, gripped the cupboard door with his snow-white teeth, pulled it open, and looped his tongue round a large glass. He flipped it up on to his scaly head and rippled his back, sending the glass sliding all the way down his spine, along his tail and into William's waiting hands.

'Thanks!' William then shoved the glass under the ice dispenser. There was a rattling sound from inside, followed by screams and cheers, then suddenly Bob, Pamela, Brenda and Santa fell out of the little hole in the freezer, bounced in and out of the glass, and expanded back into the kitchen.

Santa flung his arms up and down in a series of stretchy star jumps. 'Ah, it's good to be back to Santa-size! Right then, we still have so much to see. Follow me!' he boomed as he marched out of the kitchen.

'**Psst!**' Brenda hissed at William as Bob and Pamela hurried after Santa.

'What?' William said.

THE WINTER WITCH

'Are you thinking what I'm thinking?'

'If you're thinking that we should follow Santa and definitely not do anything stupid that'll get us into trouble, then yes,' William said.

But he knew Brenda – and he could tell that she had other plans . . .

CHAPTER NINE
FORBIDDEN

Santa led the way through the magnificently cosy Snow Ranch.

'Here's where the crumpets are delivered,' he sang. 'And over there is where the presents are wrapped.'

They reached a point where the hallway forked into two. Santa nodded cheerily down the right-hand corridor, which was brightly lit with cheery lanterns.

'Ah, now! We're almost at the place where the Christmasaurus hatched. I know you'll want to see that,' he added, smiling at William and Brenda, and the Christmasaurus growled proudly.

FORBIDDEN

'Definitely!' agreed William.

'Excellent! Bob and Pamela, perhaps you could lead the way? I just have to make a little stop – too much tasty cold milk in the kitchen,' Santa explained, patting his enormous tummy and blushing.

'We'd be honoured, Santa,' gushed Bob.

'First green door after the stocking-stitching room!' said Santa. With a nimble skip, he sprang down the shadowy left-hand corridor. Before Santa disappeared round the corner, William noticed him quickly glancing over his shoulder.

As though he doesn't want to be followed, William thought.

As Bob and Pamela walked on, chatting excitedly, William realized that Brenda had taken a quiet step after Santa. The Christmasaurus had hung back too and was watching them both curiously.

'Brenda, what are you up to?' William whispered.

'Is it just me, or is Santa acting a bit odd?' she hissed. 'And I don't mean the jolly, merry, Christmassy kind of odd. I mean like he's not telling us something.'

William said nothing, not wanting to admit that Brenda might actually be right.

'I think there's more to this Winter Witch than he's letting on. I want to find her,' she said with a mischievous twinkle in her eyes.

'You'll end up back on the Naughty List,' warned William. The Christmasaurus huffed through his nostrils in agreement.

'Well, that mouldy old tree seems to think I'm still on it anyway!' retorted Brenda, sticking her tongue out at them both. 'Fine – have it *your* way.'

She paused for a moment, then her eyes opened wide. 'Hey, William – listen! Your dad's calling you. He must have noticed we've fallen behind!'

William looked at the green door through which his dad and Pamela had disappeared. He frowned, craning his head to listen. But there was no shouting, no calling, no laughter – nothing.

Just the swift patter of footsteps behind him.

William's head whipped back.

Brenda had gone.

FORBIDDEN

'**Ugh**, did I really just fall for that? *You can take the child off the Naughty List . . .*' William sighed, shaking his head. 'What should we do, Christmasaurus?'

A chilly breeze caught the wisps of hair on the back of William's neck. The light gust came from the corridor leading off to the left.

He edged forward and looked down it.

The Christmasaurus shivered.

It was cold and gloomy, and William really, *really*, **REALLY** didn't want to go down there, and would have turned round in a heartbeat if it weren't for the flash of perfect blonde twirls scurrying away into the shadows at the far end of the dark corridor.

'Brenda . . .' he whispered.

He glanced back at the warm, happy, totally unspooky right-hand hallway and the inviting green door. His dad and Pamela would be waiting for them on the other side right now.

William sighed.

There was only one thing for it. Witch or no witch, he was going to have to go after Brenda.

135

He looked at the Christmasaurus and the blue dinosaur nodded.

They were in this together. They both set off down the left-hand hallway as quickly and quietly as they could.

'We'll grab Brenda and bring her back. We'll only be gone for a couple of minutes. No one will notice,' William told the Christmasaurus as they raced into the shadows.

The long hallway bent round to the left, and the further William headed down it, the colder it seemed to get.

Forbidden

He could see his breath on the air as he panted, and his fingers started to go numb as he pushed as hard as he could – and was it just his imagination or were the walls starting to frost up around him? And why was it getting more difficult to steer his wheelchair, almost as though he were moving through snow?

All of a sudden, he heard the slow creak of an old door swinging open up ahead.

'Whoa, whoa! Slow down!' he whispered to the Christmasaurus as the hallway led them to a large moonlit glass conservatory, which looked out over an icy garden. The wide panels on the ceiling were covered in thick snow, and the wicker garden furniture had a glistening layer of frost, which made the freezing room sparkle an eerie blue colour.

William put his finger to his lips, telling the Christmasaurus to stay silent.

Something moved in the conservatory.

William and the Christmasaurus were not alone.

Brenda crept out from behind one of the conservatory chairs and slunk towards the door at the back of the room on her tiptoes, reaching out for the brass door handle.

'BRENDA!' William barked.

Brenda leapt with fright. 'You idiot! You scared the life out of me!' she snapped.

'That's because you're up to no good!' William said as he and the Christmasaurus moved out of the darkness. 'Back to your old tricks again!'

'I'm not up to any *tricks*. The Winter Witch is through this door, and I've got to see her with my own eyes,' Brenda said.

'Why? Why are you so obsessed with seeing her when you know it's forbidden?' William asked.

'I . . . I don't know. I can't explain it. I just feel like I'm supposed to see her,' Brenda said.

'And you're sure she's through this door?'

'Yes! Look!'

Brenda pointed at the door. William looked closer and saw that there was some writing engraved on a panel above the brass handle.

THE FORBID DEN

'The Forbid Den? What on earth is that?' William asked, screwing up his face.

'Don't you get it? Sub-Zero said Santa had already told us where the Winter Witch was – and he had.'

'Santa said it was forbidden . . .' William recalled.

Then it suddenly clicked.

FORBID DEN!' he gasped.

'Exactly. The Winter Witch is through there!' Brenda said, raising her hand to turn the door handle.

The Christmasaurus let out a nervous little roar.

'Brenda, don't!' William said.

'Listen, Willypoos, this is a once-in-a-lifetime trip.'

'No, it isn't. I've been here twice.'

'Well, we can't all be BFFs with Santa's pet dinosaur!' The Christmasaurus huffed with a frown.

'What's that supposed to mean?' William snapped.

'It means I'm going through this door and seeing what this Winter Witch is all about.'

'No, you're not!' William

shouted, wheeling himself in between Brenda and the door.

'Get out of the way!'

Brenda yelled, reaching past William and gripping the door handle.

'No! Santa said not to – and the Christmasaurus has a really bad feeling about this!' William cried, grabbing Brenda's arm.

The Christmasaurus gripped Brenda's cardigan with his teeth and tried to pull her away from the door. The three of them pushed and pulled, all trying to get the upper hand. Finally, Brenda gave an almighty heave with all her strength – and the door was flung inwards.

Brenda lost her footing and stumbled forward with it, pulling the Christmasaurus with her, and they both fell on William. The momentum of the opening door, and the weight of Brenda and the dinosaur, tipped his wheelchair over the edge of the door frame.

'**Uh-oh!**' he said as they rolled through into freezing air and began hurtling down a smooth, icy path.

'**I can't stop!**'

William cried as his chair picked up speed.

'Hold on – we're going to CRASH!'

Brenda screamed, looking over William's shoulder at a fast-approaching row of snow-covered trees . . . as they crashed into the mysterious Forbid Den.

CHAPTER TEN
A-*MAZE*-ING!

His head totally submerged in snow, William could see nothing but white. Close by, he heard the soft padding of dinosaur feet on snow – the Christmasaurus was on his feet first!

'In here!' he shouted, and within a moment his dino companion was scooping him and his overturned wheelchair out of the snowdrift.

'Thanks!' William said. 'You OK?'

The Christmasaurus nodded.

'A little help here?' a muffled voice interrupted.

A few metres away, two feet were poking out of a

snow mound and William heard the frustrated, stroppy huffs of a stuck Brenda.

The Christmasaurus buried his head in the snow pile and pulled her free.

'Thanks,' Brenda breathed, brushing the snow off with a shiver.

The Christmasaurus nodded in a *you're welcome* sort of way.

'Sorry about what I said before. I didn't mean it,' Brenda said, looking genuinely sorry.

The dinosaur rubbed his head on her shoulder and William could see that she was forgiven.

'Are you OK?' Brenda asked, turning to him.

'Yeah. *That* is exactly why I always wear my seat belt!' he said. 'How about you?'

'I'm fine.'

They both nodded at each other in that same *you're welcome* sort of way. Then Brenda glanced behind William.

'Look!' she whispered.

They were staring up at a row of tall, frosted holly hedges that stretched out in both directions, as far as any of them could see. Directly in front of them was an opening cut into the holly hedge, and the frozen path they had slid down beckoned them inside.

'It's a maze,' William said, peering into the entrance.

'I think *she's* in there,' Brenda whispered.

The Christmasaurus whimpered.

'It's OK – don't be scared,' William reassured him, reaching out to pat his friend's icy mane. The truth was that *he* was totally petrified too, but there was no way he was going to let Brenda see that.

'We can do it if we work together,' Brenda said, stepping forward towards the start of the maze.

'Are you kidding? I'm not going in there. We'll get lost for sure!' William protested.

'Not with him we won't,' Brenda said, pointing at the Christmasaurus, who ducked behind William.

'What do you mean?'

'He's *a flying dinosaur*! If we get lost, he can fly into the air and help us!' she said. At that, the Christmasaurus lifted his scaly head with pride at the thought of being useful on this quest, even though William knew the dinosaur was still terrified.

A-MAZE-ING!

'OK – we'll go in for two minutes, and then we'll come straight back,' he told Brenda, trying to sound firm.

A few moments later, they were entering the maze with the Christmasaurus hovering silently overhead, just high enough to see the maze from above.

'See anything?' Brenda whispered up to him.

He shook his head and they moved on. The Christmasaurus nervously led them round the maze, guiding them through a complicated sequence of left and right turns, showing William and Brenda where to avoid the dead ends.

They were in there for what felt like hours, turning left then right, then right and left, the flying dinosaur never hesitating.

Until – suddenly – the Christmasaurus stopped dead in the air.

His scales flattened down and he sank low, so that only his eyes were peeping over the top of the holly hedge.

'What is it?' Brenda whispered.

'Can you see someone?' William asked.

The Christmasaurus nodded.

'Is it . . . her?' Brenda asked.

But right at that moment they heard a familiar voice. They froze and listened.

'I've done as you asked,' Santa said – and William had never heard the huge, jolly man sound so serious and solemn before. 'They're here. But – but are you doubly sure this is the only way?'

There was silence.

'And no one will get hurt? Cross your icicles and hope to melt?'

Silence again, and then Santa gave a deep sigh.

'Very well then . . .' he said.

William glanced at Brenda, whose mouth had dropped wide open.

'Do you think he's talking to her?' she whispered. 'What do you think all that meant?'

William shrugged. How was he to know?

Suddenly they heard the heavy thud of Santa's footsteps approaching.

'He's coming!' Brenda hissed, and in a moment of

panic she leapt into the holly-tree walls of the maze, and William had no choice but to follow her. Overhead, they heard the soft *Swoooosh* of the Christmasaurus flying out of sight above the hedges, and just in time too, as Santa trudged past them.

William caught a flash of his round, usually cheery face and realized that Santa was deep in troubled thought; he would probably have walked straight past them even if they hadn't been hiding among the branches.

A few seconds later the soft click of the conservatory door echoed through the maze and the trio of trespassers sighed in relief.

'**Ouch!**' William winced as he brushed holly leaves out of his hair.

'Sorry, I just didn't want us to get caught yet. We have to find out who he was talking to!' Brenda said excitedly.

'You've missed doing this sort of thing, haven't you?' he said.

'Yes, and you're terrible at it. Come on – let's go!' she said, marching forward. 'You should go first,' she said to William as they approached the centre of the maze.

'You've got to be kidding!'

William replied. 'You were the one who wanted to do this, Brenda!'

'Or the Christmasaurus? You're a dinosaur – you're not scared of anything, are you?'

But the Christmasaurus was trembling so much that his icy mane was jingling.

'OK, OK, I'll do it!' Brenda huffed.

She took a deep breath (and everyone reading this should probably do the same).

'One . . .
two . . .
three!'

Brenda said to herself, before stepping round the hedge.

Silence.

William stayed back, waiting to
hear if Brenda had made it.

More silence.

The Christmasaurus and the Winter Witch

The Christmasaurus whimpered nervously.

'There's no one here!' Brenda finally called. Then she added, 'Oh, wow! You two *have* to come and see this!'

William and the Christmasaurus glanced at each other and shrugged – then followed Brenda into the unknown.

When they rounded the corner, they found themselves in a glistening, snow-covered courtyard in the middle of the maze. Brenda was standing at the edge of a small, frozen fountain. The white marble basin was shaped like a large snowflake, and in the very centre, on a plinth, stood a beautiful, life-sized ice sculpture.

It was impossible for any of them to tell exactly how old the icy figure was supposed to be. She was ageless, timeless, but she was magnificent nonetheless.

She was perfectly transparent, almost as though she were carved from glass or diamonds rather than ice, and, as the moonlight shone through her, it splintered and fractured into thousands of new moonbeams that sliced through the still air of the courtyard.

She was standing with one arm out to the side, the other delicately holding a small goblet, which was totally iced over and dripping with solid icicles as she

held it to her translucent lips, as though taking a sip of tea.

Iced tea!

'Wow! I've never seen an ice sculpture like this before,' William gasped, admiring the intricate details. Each strand of hair had been perfectly chiselled into place. The woman's ageless features were so precise and particular, her movements so slow and . . .

Wait.

MOVEMENTS?!

William let out a little yelp.

The Christmasaurus leapt for cover.

Brenda froze in fright.

The ice sculpture was **alive!**

She delicately twisted her head and lowered her gaze to the side of the fountain, where William noticed that the vial containing Sub-Zero's concoction had been placed.

Ever so slowly, the living ice sculpture glided down, reached out her hand and traced a perfect circle on the icy surface of the frozen pool of her fountain. The ice obeyed her touch and dissolved away under her fingertips, revealing the chilly liquid below. Then she took the vial of potion, uncorked it and poured the glowing contents into the hole. The water below hissed like some sort of magical chemical experiment. Once the reaction had settled, she dipped her icy goblet into the hole, filling it to the brim with the blue potion, then put it to her mouth and drank.

As she swallowed, the glowing liquid could be seen through her translucent features, making its way down her throat, and creating a network of what looked like veins and arteries as it flowed through her body.

Suddenly her forehead frosted over and her frozen hair started to emit a subtle blue glow.

'William, what's happening?' Brenda whispered, barely brave enough to speak.

'I think . . . I think she's giving herself a brain freeze!' William said, trembling.

'You mean that *she* – the ice sculpture – is the Winter Witch?' Brenda gasped.

At the mention of her name, the Winter Witch's eyes locked on to Brenda, as though hearing her speak had awoken something inside.

Brenda screamed and backed away as the Winter Witch marched across the frozen fountain with terrifying purpose, reaching out for Brenda with her freezing fingers. The snow under her icy feet became solid and frozen with each step. Tiny shards of ice splintered off her body as she walked, then re-formed like icicles from a dripping pipe.

William felt helpless! How do you stop a witch made of ice?

'Do something!' he pleaded to the trembling dinosaur, who was huddled behind him. 'You're a dinosaur! People are meant to be afraid of *you*, not the other way round!'

But the Christmasaurus was frozen to the spot, utterly terrified. So William did the only thing he could do.

'Leave my sister alone!'

he screamed at the top of his lungs.

'I thought you said I was your *step*sister?' Brenda shouted.

'Now's really not the time, Brenda!' William snapped.

As the Winter Witch closed in on Brenda, the clouds

above the Forbid Den grew fearsome, as though the Winter Witch were harnessing the force of her frozen mind to conjure up a snowstorm.

William couldn't just watch. He spun his wheels as hard as he could, launching himself in front of Brenda, and blocking the Winter Witch's path.

'Leave – her – alone,' he repeated, more quietly this time, his voice trembling.

He instantly regretted it.

The Winter Witch stopped dead in her tracks and slowly turned her icy head to face him . . .

CHAPTER ELEVEN
THUNDERSNOW

T he Winter Witch towered over William, glaring into his eyes with her piercing, icy stare. It was one of the strangest experiences of William's life. It wasn't just the fact that he was staring into the crystal-like eyes of a powerful witch made entirely of ice. Somehow he had the strangest, eeriest feeling that he'd looked into these eyes before.

And, judging by the Witch's troubled expression, she was thinking the same thing.

The swirling storm above them suddenly thundered down, and the witch launched herself at William, whipping up a flurry of frost and snow as she moved. It swirled into the air, creating a small but powerful blizzard in the courtyard.

'What's happening?' Brenda screamed from somewhere in the raging snowstorm.

'I don't know!' William replied, unable to see her at all now as he desperately tried to move backwards, away from the approaching witch. It was no use. In a flash of blue, she was right in front of him. She brought one cold hand down and gripped William's arm. The chill from her touch surged through him and instantly made his skin unthinkably cold.

'**Christmasaurus, help!**' William yelled.

The dinosaur let out a panicked howl, but William couldn't see anything now. It was a total white-out all around him. He peered over his shoulder and could just about make out a fierce determination on the witch's face as she grabbed the push handles of his wheelchair. Then she flicked one hand in front of them, and the snow piled itself up and froze to form a ramp.

'Wait! Where are we going?' William asked, terrified

she was going to dump him on the frozen water. 'Wheelchairs and ice do not mix!'

But the Winter Witch kept going as though she hadn't heard him or didn't care. Either way, they were heading towards the fountain.

The blizzard stepped up a gear. William had to hold his hand up to shield his eyes from the bitter wind that swirled around them.

With a single swift movement, the witch pushed William up the ramp and on to the frozen water. She suddenly let go, letting him slide softly over the ice. William tried to wheel himself back to the edge, but it was no use. The more he tried, the more the tyres just slipped and skidded.

The Winter Witch stepped up into her place in the centre of the fountain, looking down on William.

'What are you doing?' he called, trying to get her to hear him over the howling blizzard, but still she ignored him.

Then she closed her eyes, raised her hands and softly placed her fingers on the sides of her head. The second her fingertips touched her temples, everything stopped.

The blizzard became a frozen wall of white surrounding them.

The snowflakes hung in the air as though dangling on invisible strings.

The sound had been sucked away.

It was just like the magic that had frozen the garden that morning. It was so quiet that William could hear his heartbeat thudding in his eardrums.

The Winter Witch seemed to have frozen too. She stood perfectly still atop her marble plinth. If William was ever going to escape, it had to be now! He reached down to give his wheels one final spin – but something happened that made that thudding in his ears skip a beat.

The sound came from the ice around him.

'Not good,' he whispered to himself. 'OK, Willypoos. Don't . . . move . . .'

163

This time he felt it as well as heard it. The vibration shuddered through the ice and round the metal frame of his chair.

He glanced up at the witch. She was his only hope.

'Please, help me! If the ice cracks, I'll fall in!' he cried.

The frozen witch suddenly opened her eyes.

They had changed.

They were no longer as clear as glass. They were a piercing blue, and seemed to be glowing.

The witch stood with her arms out to the side, like a diver standing at the edge of a diving board, about to jump.

'No!' William screamed, but it was no use. The Winter Witch leapt into the air, tucking her legs up under her body into a perfect cannonball. She came bombing down on to the ice, which instantly shattered into a billion shards under William, causing them both to fall . . .

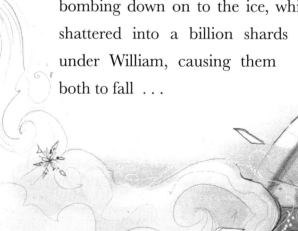

William instinctively closed his eyes and held his breath, expecting to plunge into ice-cold water, but the water never came. His stomach lurched as he fell; it was as though he had fallen off an enormously high cliff.

The fountain can't be this deep, he thought to himself.

He opened his eyes and found that he was no longer in the courtyard, and he certainly wasn't falling into a fountain of icy water. He was falling into a new place entirely, surrounded by heavy bubbling clouds. They lit up in flashes of blue thundersnow that illuminated the swirling moments around him.

Through gaps in the clouds, he heard familiar voices. Santa, Brenda, Pamela, his dad . . .

'Help!' he called, but his voice was a whisper in the vastness of this place.

William was falling head first now. He looked all around for the Winter Witch, but she was nowhere up ahead. Suddenly a piercing blue light shone from over his shoulder. He looked back and saw that the witch was behind him again, guiding him onward.

They advanced through the mass of heaving and swelling clouds. The Winter Witch pushed forward

with purpose now, never averting her gaze. Wherever she was taking William, it was as though she had something important to show him.

William saw a break in the storm; it was towards this that the witch was heading. As they closed in, the clouds did too, and it felt to William like being wrapped in a heavy, freezing blanket. Snowflakes pelted his face, wind rushed through his hair, and the witch pressed on, lighting the way with the glow of her eyes.

The storm was relentless.

Heavier.

Faster.

Stronger.

'Make . . . it . . . **STOP!!!!**' William screamed, and, in the crack of a walnut, everything stopped.

William was covered from head to toe in snow, but at least he seemed to be upright. He tried to move, but his wheels felt stuck to the . . .

'Ground!' he whispered, realizing that he wasn't falling any more.

Puff! He punched one fist out of the snow. He felt cool air on the other side. He could do this!

Puff! He smashed his other fist through.

THUNDERSNOW

He wriggled and shook until the snow around him fell away, revealing Thistle Lane – the gloomy, empty alleyway in which we saw William Trundle right at the very beginning of this book.

William was in the future!

CHAPTER TWELVE
BACK TO THE PROLOGUE

As you may well have guessed, this is the very same spot that you read about at the beginning, where William saw the bustling future city streets full of future business people on their way to their future jobs, with flying future cars soaring on the busy skyway, all in the shadow of that giant letter P looking down from the top of the tallest starscraper.

William understood that this was London, but not as he knew it. The loose-flying newspaper landed at his feet and he read the date – it was Christmas Day in London, THIRTY years in the future!

BACK TO THE PROLOGUE

The Winter Witch had brought him there. But why?

He suddenly heard the secret carollers singing in the shadows, then saw them hiding from the Christmas Police as they appeared in the sky to shut down the forbidden carol service.

Then William watched as the old caroller rebelled against the Christmas Ban with his musical Christmas knitwear, and was thrown into the back of the police car – and, as you already know, that man was Bob Trundle. William's dad!

William didn't mean to scream **'DAD!'** but it just came out, giving away his hiding place by the rubbish bin. William felt like his mind was splitting in two.

'Save your dad, William!' said one half.

'Get out of here now!' replied the other. 'You can't do anything about this mess if you end up in prison too!'

William groaned. 'Would you two stop arguing? This is no time to – Hang on a second!'

The two halves of William's mind had given him a thought. *I just travelled through time! I can just go back and warn Dad about the future and then this will never happen!* he realized.

'Take me back, **NOW!**' he screamed at the witch, who had been watching from the shadows with no reaction, no emotion, as though she had seen it all before.

Just as the Christmas Police surrounded William's hiding spot, the Winter Witch whipped up an instant blizzard. Everything and everyone around him froze again and he found himself watching the scene as if it were in a snow globe. The stillness lasted only a moment before the chaotic storm of time travel resumed and pulled them back into the swirling vortex of time.

As they fell, or flew, or whatever it was they were doing, William saw future London fade away behind a gap in the snowstorm. A few seconds later, another break in the clouds opened up and, in a great flash of thundersnow, William caught sight of something utterly amazing.

Himself!

It was last year, on the day he posted his letter to Santa. His dad was helping him pop the letter into the postbox of the past, right before his eyes!

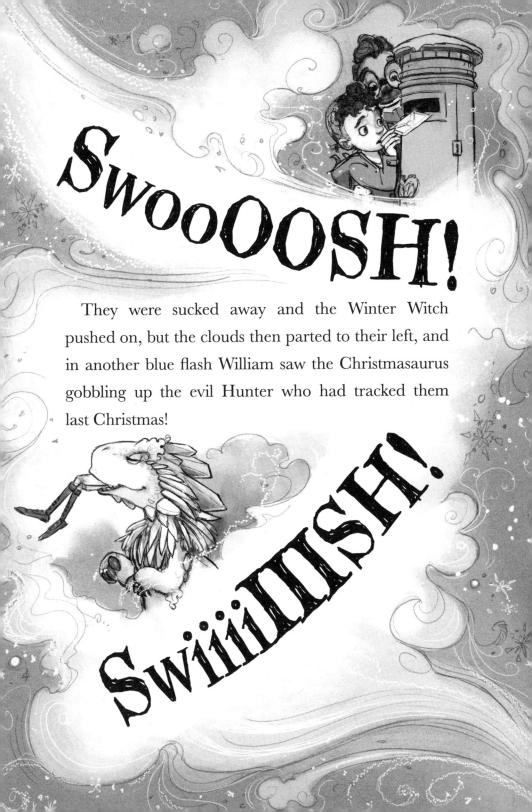

SwooOOSH!

They were sucked away and the Winter Witch pushed on, but the clouds then parted to their left, and in another blue flash William saw the Christmasaurus gobbling up the evil Hunter who had tracked them last Christmas!

SwiiiiUUSH!

THE CHRISTMASAURUS AND THE WINTER WITCH

The moment vanished again, and they fell onward as another gap opened above them, then another below, until there were cracks in the storm clouds all around them, letting in sounds and scenes from William's past.

He glimpsed his dad dancing with Pamela last Christmas . . .

William and the Christmasaurus escaping from the museum . . .

and even the Christmasaurus hatching from his frozen egg at the North Pole!

Back to the Prologue

These moments flashed by, just out of reach. William tried to hang on to them, but the blizzard around them was growing. He glanced back at the Winter Witch and saw that she was clinging on to his wheelchair with one hand while rubbing the side of her icy head with the other, almost as though she were wincing with pain.

A swell in the clouds of time rose up from below, lifting William's chair like a boat on a wave.

'Whoa!'

he yelled as the waves ebbed and flowed, causing his stomach to leap into his chest.

Then a gust of crosswind caught them off guard, sending them both into a spin.

'What's . . . happening . . .?' William strained as the force of the storm had him clinging on for dear life. He looked back at the Winter Witch, and gasped.

The bright blue glow from the witch's eyes was flickering and fading behind him. Was her magical brain freeze wearing off?

'Don't let go! Don't let go!' he begged, but the storm was too strong, even for the Winter Witch. With the next surge, he saw the thing he had been dreading: the Winter Witch's grip failed. Her icy fingers slipped away from the dinosaur grips on his wheelchair handles, and he tumbled into the vortex.

William was falling through time!

'HEEEEELP!'

he screamed, but there was no one but him in the blizzard now. He was falling helplessly, with no way of knowing where or when he was going to end up!

All of a sudden, William spotted a break in the clouds. A cool light was shining beyond in what looked like a large, empty room. He stretched with all his might, desperately spinning his wheels in the direction of this little gap in time. The snowflakes spun around him, almost as though they were obeying his command. He hurtled nearer and nearer, and . . .

BACK TO THE PROLOGUE

William landed in a long, empty corridor.

He shook off the snow that had fallen out of the storm with him and glanced around. 'Hello?' he called, his voice echoing off the pale green walls.

'Keep it down, please – it's the middle of the night!' whispered a woman in a pale blue uniform, wheeling a trolley of food past him.

'Excuse me,' William called in his best loud whisper. 'Where am I?'

The woman stopped and scrunched up her face, looking concerned. 'You're at Holly Fields Hospital, my dear. My name is Nurse Rita. Are you lost?'

William wasn't sure what to say. He could hardly say, *Yes, I was just travelling through time with a frozen witch who kidnapped me from the North Pole where I was visiting Santa, along with my dinosaur friend.*

But thankfully something interrupted him, which meant he didn't have to say anything at all.

'My Willypoos!' a voice sang out from further down the hospital corridor.

William's heart leapt. That was his dad – and Dad would be able to help him work out what to do next!

'I'm fine, actually. That's my dad!' William said to the worried-looking nurse.

'Are you sure?' Nurse Rita asked.

'Trust me. Unless there's someone else called *Willypoos* in this hospital?' William smiled.

Nurse Rita chuckled.

'OK, well, go straight to your father, young man, and keep the noise down in future. This is the maternity ward, you know!'

William nodded and moved away in the direction of his dad's voice. He passed closed door after closed door, hearing the occasional whimper or coo of a baby on the other side. At the far end of the corridor, a shaft of light leaked out from an open door and William saw shadows moving beyond.

As he got nearer, he heard his father speak again, and he felt all his worries disappear. Somehow, in all the swirling time-travel madness, he'd managed to get back home!

But why was his dad in a hospital?

'William,' Bob said. 'William Trundle.'

William was about to wheel himself through the

door and say, *Right here, Dad . . .*

. . . but someone else spoke first.

'How many times are you going to say his name?' a woman said from somewhere in the room.

William slowed himself down and paused outside the doorway. Who was his dad talking to?

He carefully peered through the crack in the open door so that he couldn't be seen, and what he saw inside made the world pause for a moment.

His dad was pacing the small room, cradling a tiny baby in his arms. William spotted a tuft of curly brown hair protruding from the bundle of blue blanket.

'William Trundle,' his dad whispered again with pride.

'Our little Willypoos!' came the woman's voice again with a chuckle, and as his dad stepped out of the way William saw *her* lying in the hospital bed.

He didn't need to be told who she was. He knew it instantly.

William was looking at his mother.

She looked exhausted, but she was still the most beautiful woman he had ever seen.

Cold hands suddenly wrapped round him, ripping him away from the moment.

'No!' William cried. 'Let me see her! Let me stay!'

But the moment was fading into the storm clouds once again as the Winter Witch pulled him out of the past. She held on to William tightly. They were falling faster now. William closed his eyes and a single tear escaped and froze instantly in the air.

He'd always dreamt of meeting his mother again, wondering what he'd say, what he'd do.

BACK TO THE PROLOGUE

Without warning, they collapsed out of the swirling blizzard, back into the frozen courtyard of the Forbid Den. The snow settled around them and William's chair came to rest at the foot of the snowflake-shaped fountain.

'Been anywhere interesting, young William?' boomed Santa's voice.

His head spinning, his teeth still chattering from the frozen storm, William looked up to see Brenda and the Christmasaurus watching him anxiously as they stood next to Santa.

In any other circumstances, William would have felt so guilty for breaking the rules and letting Santa down – but the only thing going through his mind was the image of his mother.

'William? Are you OK?' Brenda asked. 'You've gone so pale!'

'My dear child, you look as though you've seen a ghost,' Santa said gently, placing a hand on William's shoulder.

'I think . . . maybe I did,' William said.

CHAPTER THIRTEEN
ONE MORE STOP

'I heard my dad's voice saying my name. I thought he was calling me at first, but when I got there I realized he wasn't really speaking to me. Well, he was, just not *me*-me. He was talking to young me, little me . . . me as a BABY! I think it must have been the day I was born!'

William was trying to explain what had happened to Santa, Brenda and the Christmasaurus, who were all having a hard time trying to keep up.

'That's when I noticed her lying in bed in the hospital. It was my mum!'

'But how do you know it was her?' Brenda said. 'Didn't your mum die when you were really little?'

'Yes, but I just knew the moment I saw her. She looked exactly like the photos Dad has.'

'Are you sure you weren't dreaming? Maybe you bumped your head when the witch grabbed you?' Brenda suggested.

The witch! William had almost forgotten about her. He turned to look at the moonlit fountain and saw that the witch had resumed her position in the centre, her goblet held to her lips as though elegantly taking a sip.

'*Grabbed* you?' Santa asked.

William nodded.

Santa looked up at the witch and cocked his head.

'What is it?' asked Brenda.

Santa turned and looked deep into Brenda's eyes with an expression that suggested the cogs of his mind were busy figuring something out, as though they were on the cusp of solving a riddle.

'I've never known the Winter Witch to do that before,' he explained slowly. 'She doesn't need to touch someone to transport them through time. She's so powerful that she can simply move people through the days, the months, the years, with just her mind . . . Why she decided to grab *you*, William, I really don't know.'

Brenda frowned, and the Christmasaurus gave a troubled little whimper. But William's thoughts were already racing ahead.

'Santa, do you think I could see her again? My mum, I mean. Just for a second?' he asked, although he thought he might already know the answer.

Santa placed a warm hand on William's shoulder, but his voice was still low and serious. 'William, my dear young thing,' he said kindly. 'Time is as complicated and fragile as a snowflake. If you handle it carelessly, a snowflake will melt, and its beautiful structure will be lost. Time is not something for us to go wandering into willy-nilly.'

'But I promise I won't touch anything. I won't even speak to her. I'll just watch!' William said desperately.

'William, freezing time can change people permanently! Just look at the Winter Witch here.'

'You mean she was . . . a *person* once?' Brenda said in disbelief.

'I believe so, but a person who meddled with time so much she became frozen in it, living every moment simultaneously.'

Santa sighed as William's shoulders slumped in disappointment. 'I'm sorry, William, but if you were to accidentally change something in the past – even something small – it could have a disastrous effect on the future.'

The future.

The words suddenly rang like an alarm in William's head.

'I almost forgot! The witch took me there too!' he burst out.

'Where?' Brenda asked.

'To the future! And there's something I've *got* to tell you, Santa. Christmas might depend on it!' William said.

'Absolutely NOT!' Santa boomed, his voice causing snow to topple from the surrounding trees.

William stared. 'But, Santa, it's –'

'No!' Santa interrupted.

'It's about Christmas,' William tried to tell him again, but Santa put his hands over his ears.

'I don't want to hear a single thing about the future, William!' he shouted. 'No one should! It hasn't happened yet.'

'It *will* happen, though, and I've seen what it is!' William said.

One More Stop

'And now you'll be *expecting* it to happen that way, which makes it even more likely to become a reality,' Santa told him.

'Huh?' Brenda screwed up her face, totally confused.

'If someone tells you how a book is going to end, then you will find it ends exactly as you are expecting. However, before you were told the ending, that book had a billion different possibilities, and the ending was yours to discover. If you tell us what you saw, William, the chances are we will make that future happen, because we *know* it will happen,' Santa explained.

'But what if I know something bad will happen in the future, Santa? Shouldn't I do something about it?' William asked.

'William, there is always the possibility of bad things happening in the future. The only way to stop them coming true is to do something about the bad things *right now*. The present moment is all we need to focus on. Why do you think they're called Christmas *presents*? They're not called Christmas futures or Christmas pasts, are they?'

William and Brenda thought about that for a moment, trying to make sense of it all.

'Now, may I suggest that we get you back to your parents? Sub-Zero mixed that extra teacup of potion for the Winter Witch so that she could keep the rest of the world frozen in time just a little longer while you were here at the North Pole. Now that she's used it up on this – er, *unexpected* time-travelling trip with you, William, I'm not sure how much longer things back home will stay frozen. So let's skedaddle! And pretty please with a ribbon on top, keep this little episode to yourselves. People have a terrible tendency to be very curious about the past and the future, and it leads to nothing but trouble.'

'But the thing I saw in the future – it affects my dad too,' William explained.

'Even more reason to keep it to yourself then, William!' Santa said, ushering him and Brenda out of the courtyard.

As they left, William caught Santa stealing one final searching glance at the Winter Witch, as though trying to work something out. Then he guided them back through the maze and found Bob and Pamela waiting for them at the entrance.

'Where have you two been?' Pamela said with folded arms.

'Did you see anything else Christmassy?' whispered Bob.

William glanced at Brenda.

'Just more books,' she lied.

All of a sudden, a fanfare of trumpets blasting from somewhere beyond the snow-topped conservatory caused the windows to burst open, and the children had to cover their ears.

'Goodness gracious, great baubles of fire, that's loud!' Santa cried. 'Ah, and I'm afraid that sound means that our tour really has come to an end. That's the elves telling me I'm needed back at the Snow Ranch – I've got to check the Naughty and Nice Lists for the eighty-seventh time, just to be sure.'

'Can't we stay a tiny bit longer?' Bob asked hopefully.

'I think you've seen all that you can see on this trip – but don't worry, Bob. You're always welcome here at the North Pole – and the same goes for all of you! Now let's get you all back home. To the sleigh!' Santa announced.

'I totally forgot about the sleigh!' said Pamela.

'And the tiny elf city!' added Bob blissfully.

'And the glowing wishes in the forest!' said Pamela.

'And the sprite in the fridge with the secret potion,' William said.

'And the secret witch made of ice who kidnapped you and took you on a trip through time . . .' Brenda whispered to him.

'And, of course, a flying blue dinosaur!' he said quickly, in case anyone had overheard Brenda. The Christmasaurus hopped with happiness and let out a little roar of joy.

'This place is the chestnuts!' said Brenda, punching the air.

They followed Santa back to the open snowfield where his eight magical reindeer were having their final pre-flight checks carried out by an elf called Skysafe, who ran the North Pole air-traffic control. The Christmasaurus skipped over giddily and scooped his scaly head into the harness at the front, ready to lead them all.

'All aboard the sleigh then,' Santa said, and the ramp

lowered for William, while the others leapt into their seats. Bob and Pamela squidged on to the seat next to Santa, and Brenda and William rode in the toy-cargo area again.

The whole flight back to London, Bob, Pamela and Brenda all talked excitedly about the wonderful things they'd seen on their tour of the North Pole. William joined in too, but, if Bob hadn't been so swept up in the excitement of the day, he might have noticed that his son was a little quieter than usual. William's mind kept returning to the fountain of ice, those bright blue eyes, and the crash of the thundersnow as he fell through time . . .

'**Psst!**' Brenda hissed, getting his attention.

'What?' he whispered.

'Do you know what you're going to ask your magic bean for yet?' she asked.

William had forgotten all about it, until now. 'Not yet,' he said.

'Ugh! That bean is wasted on you. I had loads of brilliant ideas,' huffed Brenda. 'I'd already decided what I was going to ask for.'

'What?' William asked.

Brenda shook her head. 'Not telling!'

'Why not?'

'I can't!'

'Brenda, if it's really bad, maybe that's why the tree wouldn't give it to you,' said William.

'It wasn't bad! It was just a loophole.'

'A loophole?' blurted out William.

One More Stop

'Shh, keep it down! I don't think I would have been breaking too many rules . . . Anyway, it doesn't matter now,' Brenda finished, shrugging.

William reached into his pocket and found his Christmas bean pod, snuggled up next to the fluffy wish he'd adopted. He pulled it out, turning it over in his hands. In his head, he heard Santa's voice . . . *the gift of whatever you want.*

There was only one thing William wanted. To travel back in time again, and see his . . .

Suddenly the bean wobbled ever so slightly in his hands, and William had the strange feeling that it was listening to his thoughts, trying to hear what he wanted it to become.

He quickly tucked the bean back into his pocket. He wanted to save it for when he got home, to do it properly, without Brenda watching over his shoulder.

For the rest of the flight he gazed out at the horizon, thinking about everything he'd seen in the past and wondering if he might get to see it again in the future.

CHAPTER FOURTEEN
HOME IS WHERE THE TRUTH IS

The Christmasaurus galloped across the sky above William's wonky little house. The family gazed down at the still-frozen town below.

Everything was exactly the way they had left it.

The birds were still still.

The neighbours were emotionlessly motionless.

Growler was growling silently through the window.

'Ho, ho, hold on tight!' Santa boomed from behind the reins as the Christmasaurus twisted into a vertical dive towards the garden. Santa pulled up just in the nick of time to plonk down perfectly on their small patch of lawn.

'Right, off you get – back to the first day of your Christmas holidays!' Santa said, and they all climbed out of the sleigh, sad that the trip was over.

'That was the best day of my life!' Bob sniffed, and Pamela handed him a tissue.

William went over to the Christmasaurus, whose icy mane was drooping with sadness.

'It's OK. Christmas is only a couple of weeks away – I'll see you then!' William said, stroking the dinosaur's cool skin. 'You will come in and say hello, won't you?'

The Christmasaurus nodded. He made a little rumble in his throat that sounded like a cat purr as he nestled his nose into William to say goodbye, before taking his place at the front of the sleigh.

'See you all on Christmas Eve! Remember to take good care of your Christmas bean, William. I look forward to seeing what grows from it!' Santa said.

With a tip of his hat and a blast of music from his magical golden gramophone, Santa launched the sleigh across the snowy garden and shot up into the grey sky.

As he flew away, a faint echo of singing could be heard, followed by a trickle of warmth that settled over them like drinking a mug of hot chocolate and . . .

. . . just like that . . .

. . . everything thawed.

The world was alive again. Birds fluttered, snow fell, Growler barked, and William, Brenda, Bob and Pamela glanced at each other and smiled in the way of those who share a secret.

'Well, that's one way to kick off the Christmas holidays!' said Pamela.

'It's going to be pretty hard for the rest of December to live up to that,' said Bob, turning to William, who had pulled out his magical bean and was staring at it.

'Do you wish you had one?' Pamela asked him with a smile.

'A little bit!' he admitted as they all went back inside.

'Me too,' Brenda grumbled under her breath so that only William heard her, and he slipped the bean back into his pocket.

As they entered the kitchen, Growler leapt up and greeted them.

'Down, boy!' Brenda laughed. 'I know, I'm sorry we couldn't take you.'

A high-pitched noise suddenly cut through the air; the tune loosely resembled 'We Wish You a Merry Christmas'.

'Ah! The new doorbell works!' said Bob, grinning.

'We have a Christmas doorbell?' asked Brenda.

'Installed it this morning, before you two woke up!' he explained.

'We'll have it for the rest of December!' added William. 'And a little bit of January too. Sometimes February as well if Dad really can't face taking it down.'

'Wow, I'm almost glad I'm spending it at my . . .' Brenda paused, and her face fell as the doorbell rang again.

'He's here already?' she said.

They went through to the living room and peered through the curtains – and what William saw outside made his jaw hit the floor.

It was the longest stretch limo he'd ever laid eyes on.

It must have been a

super-stretch.

Or even a

super-
duper-
stretch!

And it wasn't black like the limos William had seen before. This one was entirely gold! From the bonnet to the boot, it glistened with yellowy richness. Its midnight-black-tinted windows reflected the wonky little house,

making it look even smaller and wonkier than it actually was – which was quite impressive, as it was already pretty small and wonky.

'That car is bigger than our house!' William said.

'Well, yes, but I bet it doesn't have a Christmas doorbell,' Pamela replied, and William saw her place her hand on Bob's shoulder.

At that very moment, the horn of the enormously oversized, super-duper-stretch limo let out an enormous **HONK** and it was so loud that the whole wonky house rattled.

'I think we'd better let him in,' Pamela said, biting her lip.

'Who?' William asked.

'Dad,' Brenda replied flatly.

'Wait . . . you mean, that's your dad's car?'

Brenda nodded, her cheeks flushing. 'Do I have to go? Things are going to be so Christmassy here, and we've just had the most amazing Christmassy day, and – well, Dad's not really into it like you are,' she said, looking at Bob.

Home Is Where the Truth Is

William saw his dad's usually jolly face grow sad. He knew how much his dad enjoyed company at Christmas, and that he loved the way their little house was slowly starting to feel like a family home.

'Oh, Brenda, I'd love you to stay, but we've talked about this. He's your dad and I'm sure he's looking forward to having his little girl home for Christmas,' Bob said.

Brenda let out a long, disappointed sigh.

'I've packed a case for you, Brenda. Run along and get it from your room.' Pamela smiled encouragingly, but William saw the sadness in her eyes.

Brenda left the living room in a sulk. Even the blonde twirls in her hair looked dejected.

'I'll get the door,' Bob said, puffing out his chest a little.

'Now, William, you wait in the kitchen,' Pamela instructed.

'But can't I meet Brenda's – '

'The kitchen, Willypoos!' she said sternly.

She'd never snapped at William before and he saw her face flush instantly with regret.

'It's OK, William. It won't take long,' Bob said, nodding.

William did as he was told, but he didn't close the kitchen door entirely, leaving just enough of a gap for him to see the front door. There was no way he was going to miss this!

Bob stepped up to the front door, straightened his Christmas jumper, took a breath and opened it wide.

'Ah, so you must be —'

Before Bob could finish, Brenda's dad barged into the hallway, pushing past without even a glance at Bob. He was wearing a strangely familiar pinstripe suit and pristine, polished black shoes, and he was speaking very loudly into his phone, having some sort of argument, it seemed.

'Do you know who I am? I don't give a monkey's toenail if the entire shipment is faulty! That's the child's problem, not mine. Just get toys on the shelves and sell! Sell! SELL!' he blasted.

He marched into the living room. 'Brenda! Time to go!' he shouted, ending the phone call. 'Pamela, is that you? My goodness, you look tired. I barely recognized you. It's surprising how much someone can age in a year.'

HOME IS WHERE THE TRUTH IS

William saw Bob frown, hesitate, then follow Mr Payne into the living room, closing the door behind him. William quickly went over to the kitchen wall and placed his ear against it, trying to hear the conversation on the other side.

'Thanks. You look the same as ever,' Pamela said, managing to keep her cool.

'Well, who said money can't buy looks, eh?' Mr Payne laughed. It sounded like a duck quacking.

'This is Bob Trundle. Bob, this is Barry,' Pamela said.

Barry. So that's Brenda's dad's name. Barry Payne, William thought.

'Pleased to meet you,' Bob said politely. 'I'm glad our paths are finally crossing. Brenda is a wonderful girl –'

'Oh, are you off to a fancy-dress party then, Bobby?' Barry interrupted.

'Excuse me?'

'That awful Christmas knitwear you're wearing. You must be going to a Christmas do of some sort . . . Worst-dressed competition?'

'Oh, my jumper! It's actually my all-time favourite,' Bob said proudly, then William heard the faint sound of

'Jingle Bells' coming from the in-built speaker system in his dad's new Christmas jumper.

Suddenly there was another awful blast of duck-quacking laughter.

'PWAH-HA-HA-HA! . . . Oh!'

Barry stopped laughing. 'You're actually wearing that because you *like* it? I thought you were pulling my leg. Pamela, you aren't dating one of these Christmas addicts who put up their Christmas tree in November, are you?'

'Barry, please . . .' Pamela said.

William understood why Brenda didn't want to spend Christmas with this twerp!

HOME IS WHERE THE TRUTH IS

'Christmas is for nitwits,' Barry scoffed. 'If I had my way, I'd scrap the whole thing.'

'That's surprising, considering your line of work,' Bob said, and William could tell his dad was speaking through gritted teeth.

'Oh, so you're an expert on how to run my business, are you?' Barry snapped.

'I'm ready!' Brenda called from the hallway – and just in time, William thought. He went back to the kitchen door and peeked through the gap into the hallway. Bob came out of the living room, looking flustered and red-

cheeked, followed by Pamela, who gently rubbed his back for comfort.

'Hi, Dad,' Brenda said nervously as she stepped forward to give him the first hug in a year.

'Oh, hang on, someone's just calling me,' Barry said, fumbling in his pocket for his phone as he stepped past Brenda. 'What?!' he snapped into it. 'I told you, I don't ruddy care about the quality as long as it's on the shelves **TODAY!**'

Brenda's arms dropped and she rolled her eyes at William.

'Let's go, Brenda,' Barry said. 'I can't imagine you'd want to be here any longer than you have to. It's so *small*. And . . . wonky.'

'OK, Dad. Oh, wait! Let me just say bye to William,' Brenda said, and she walked past Bob and Pamela into the kitchen.

'You all right?' William asked.

'I'll be fine. You have a merry Christmas . . . bro!' Brenda forced a smile and opened her arms for a hug.

William laughed.

'What?' asked Brenda.

Home Is Where the Truth Is

'Since when do we do hugs?'

'Since you get to stay here while I have to spend Christmas in the least magical place in the world. Bring it in!' she said.

William smiled and Brenda leant in, giving him a tight squeeze before dragging her feet back down the hallway to the front door.

William followed and saw Brenda's dad properly for the first time as he slicked back a few strands of oily hair and straightened his tie.

'Ah, this your boy then, is it?' Barry said, spotting William.

'Yes, this is William,' replied Bob proudly.

'**HOW**

  DO

    YOU

      DO!' Barry said, loudly and slowly, as though William couldn't hear him.

'*Barry!*' Pamela hissed.

'What?' he shot back.

'It's OK. It's nice to meet you, Mr –'

William froze before he could finish the sentence.

MR P.

The cogs in his head hadn't been spinning fast enough for him to realize, but it was so obvious now. His mind leapt back to the TV at the North Pole and the awful advert they'd seen.

A grin spread over Mr Payne's face. 'Ah, you recognize me off the television, don't you, boy! A bit star-struck? Never met a real celebrity before, I assume? I get it ALL the time. Listen, you don't need to wait for that fat imbecile to come down the chimbley to get your Christmas presents. Nip by any of my extremely successful toyshops and we'll look after you. Family discount. Pwah-ha-ha! *Family!*'

He quacked to himself as he walked out of the door and snapped his fingers. A weary-looking chauffeur leapt out of the driver's seat of the limo and came scurrying over with an umbrella, so that Mr P didn't get a single snowflake on his suit. He strolled over to the passenger door, leaving Brenda to drag her own case.

'Brenda . . . your dad is the guy from those awful adverts? "*Who needs Santa?*"' William said slowly.

Home Is Where the Truth Is

'I know. I just couldn't face telling you. I'm sorry,' she whispered.

'Miss Payne, your father requests your presence in the limousine immediately,' called the chauffeur from the limo.

Pamela bent down and gave Brenda a huge, squishy mum hug. 'Ring me every day, love,' she said. 'You'll be back before you know it.'

Brenda nodded. Before she trudged away, Bob held out something he'd been hiding behind his back. It was the snow globe from the kitchen.

'Take this with you, to remind you of home.' He smiled.

Brenda looked at the cosy little hand-carved log cabin inside the snow globe and smiled back as she put it in her backpack. As she climbed inside the limo, Bob put one arm round Pamela and waved.

'Merry Chri–'

He was cut off by the roar of the engine as the golden limo raced down the street, and they watched the **MR P** number plate disappear into the distance.

Brenda was gone.

CHAPTER FIFTEEN
WHAT BRENDA WANTED

Barry Payne's new penthouse apartment was as big as a school. It was the highest, most luxurious residence in Swanky Heights, the tallest tower block in town.

As one of Mr Payne's terrified staff opened the door, Brenda stepped inside with her case and looked around. From the entrance hall, she could see a chilly-looking dining room, a swimming pool, a plunge pool, a saltwater pool, a golf simulator, an indoor putting green and a library of books with titles like *Making Money for Beginners* and *Get Rich, Get Happy* and *Happy Bank Balance,*

What Brenda Wanted

Happy Dad. Huge white vases filled with expensive-looking flowers filled every corner. A chandelier hung from the high ceiling, and thick grey blinds covered the panoramic windows.

A year ago, I would have thought this place was amazing, Brenda thought, thinking sadly of the warm, wonky little house she'd woken up in that morning.

'This is where you live now?' she asked her dad.

'This shabby old loft? Just temporarily! Temporarily!' he said, waving his hands dismissively. 'It's just a pied-à-terre while I'm having the manor renovated.'

'A pied-à-*what*?' Brenda asked.

'A *pied-à-terre*!' Barry said slowly as if she were an idiot. 'All rich people have them. It means . . . well . . . it means . . .'

Brenda looked at him, waiting for a definition.

'It means I've got loads of money. Enough for a second place, OK!' he scoffed.

Brenda still couldn't get used to hearing her dad say things like *pied-à-terre* and *manor renovated*. Ever since his toy business had boomed a few years ago, he'd changed. He became selfish where he'd once been kind, ignorant where he used to be so understanding.

Money had transformed Barry Payne, and not for the better!

That's the thing about money: once some people have it, all they seem to want is more.

As Barry walked around his apartment, showing it off to Brenda, his staff removed his suit jacket, untied his tie, swapped his shoes for slippers, placed his reading

glasses on his nose, put an espresso in one hand and a newspaper in the other. All without him even batting an eyelid.

'Nice, eh? Must be an improvement on that rat-infested place you've been living in! Now I bet you're hungry,' Barry said, sipping his black coffee and sitting on the most uncomfortable-looking armchair Brenda had ever seen.

Brenda desperately wanted to scream, *It's not rat-infested and it's a nicer house than this place will ever be!* But the truth was that she *was* hungry – the last time she'd eaten was in the kitchens at the North Pole! And, she thought, yelling at her dad wasn't going to get her anywhere.

So she just said, 'Starving!'

Barry snapped his fingers and the click echoed around the huge room.

'Y-yes, sir?' panted an older lady dressed in a black dress and white apron, who had obviously run to answer his finger-snap as fast as she could.

'Mrs Buttersby, my child is hungry,' Barry said, not bothering to take his eyes off his newspaper.

Mrs Buttersby didn't move, obviously waiting for an actual instruction.

'Have you forgotten your hearing aids? Don't just stand there, Mrs Buttersby. Fetch the girl some food!' barked Barry.

'Oh! Yes, right away, sir. Sorry, sir!' Mrs Buttersby said, snapping back to life as she nervously scurried away to the kitchen.

'Actually, Dad, I might just go and see what you

have in the fridge,' Brenda said casually.

'Yes, yes, run along. Just don't touch anything expensive . . . which is basically everything!' Barry said, barely paying her any attention as he absorbed the *Financial Times*.

Brenda followed Mrs Buttersby to the kitchen. It was a glistening sight, every surface covered in polished marble.

'What would you like, dear?' Mrs Buttersby asked as she peered at Brenda through thick glasses.

'I'll just get myself a glass of water and a piece of toast. If that's OK?'

Mrs Buttersby seemed relieved. 'Help yourself, dear! Glasses are over there, and there's bread in the cupboard. Will that be all? I've got a big pile of Mr Payne's underpants to finish ironing,' she explained.

'Yes, thank you,' Brenda replied, and Mrs Buttersby left the room, giving the door handle a quick polish as she went.

The moment Mrs Buttersby disappeared, Brenda shoved her hand into her pocket and pulled out . . .

A red-and-white striped bean.

WILLIAM'S BEAN!

Her heart was racing. Of all the naughty things she had ever done, slipping this out of William's pocket as she leaned in for that goodbye hug was by far the worst!

She hadn't exactly planned to take it, but when she squeezed him it had just sort of popped out and accidentally-on-purpose fallen into her sneaky open hand . . . along with the instructions Santa had given him.

William was going to waste it, she told herself. Whereas she knew precisely what to do with it. Plus, he *did* have a wish in his pocket too. If he stopped being such a namby-pamby he could get what he wanted from that!

First things first. The bean had been stuffed in her pocket throughout the whole limo drive, and now she had to get it in the freezer.

She fumbled around in her pocket again and pulled out the little instruction card that had come with the bean.

It read:

What Brenda Wanted

1. Don't eat the bean!

2. Seriously, don't even lick it!

3. Tell the bean what you want for Christmas.

4. Place bean in freezer.

5. Sing Christmas songs to it once a day.

6. Wait for your present to grow!

Brenda smiled, thinking about her plan – the loophole – then glanced over her shoulder, fearing that Mrs Buttersby might come back at any moment. She rushed over to the freezer, opened the door, and pulled out a large drawer. She pushed some boxes aside to clear a space in the back corner, somewhere the bean wouldn't be seen.

She took a breath and was about to whisper what she wanted for Christmas when something else popped into her head, something unexpected – *William.*

He looked sad, like he'd been crying, and she realized that this was what William's face was going to look like when he reached into his empty pocket and discovered that his Christmas bean from Santa was missing.

Then what would her mum say? 'Up to your old

tricks!' she imagined Pamela's voice ringing in her mind.

And Bob? Lovely, kind, Christmassy Bob? He'd be the most disappointed of them all . . .

Her heart thumped in her chest as she stared at the glistening red stripes swirling around the bean and suddenly caught sight of her reflection in its shiny surface.

Staring back at her wasn't the Brenda she wanted to be but the Brenda of the past. Brenda who was always getting into trouble. Brenda who was on the Naughty List.

She didn't want to go back to being *that* Brenda.

'I can't do this,' she whispered to herself. 'It's not right.' And she made a promise there and then that, one way or another, she would get this bean back to William.

She carefully slid the drawer back so it wouldn't make a sound and quietly she closed the freezer door – but, as it swung shut, it revealed something awful . . .

HER DAD'S FACE!

'What have you got there?' he said with a nasty grin.

'**Dad!**' she gasped, hiding the bean behind her back.

'You were up to no good.'

'I wasn't, honest!' Brenda said, shaking her head.

Barry smiled, showing his white teeth, before snapping his fingers again. Suddenly a blank TV screen in the wall came to life. On it was footage of the kitchen from a hidden security camera. Brenda watched as Mrs Buttersby walked in, followed by herself. A few moments later, she watched herself reaching into her pocket for the Christmas bean, and . . .

SNAP!

Her dad's fingers paused the footage.

'Still want to lie to me?' he said.

The game was up. He'd been watching her the whole time!

'Don't kid a kidder, kid!' Barry said, holding out his hand expectantly. 'What are you hiding?'

Brenda's voice sounded very small as she replied, 'It's . . . it's a present.'

'A present? What sort of present do you put in the

freezer?' Barry laughed as Brenda reluctantly handed over the magical bean.

It shimmered and sparkled magically like a jewel in his carefully manicured fingertips.

'I think you'd better explain what this is, young lady,' he said, studying the bean. 'Did you steal this from someone?'

'**NO!**' Brenda lied.

'Then tell me what it is or I'll chuck it straight down the rubbish chute,' Barry snapped, pulling open a metal panel in the wall and holding the bean above it. 'And remember Swanky Heights is fifty floors high, Brenda. Whatever this thing is, it'll be smushed to a pulp by the time it lands at the bottom!'

WHAT BRENDA WANTED

'OK, OK!' Brenda screamed.

She took a deep breath. 'I know this is going to sound crazy, but that is a magical Christmas bean from the magical North Pole that came from a magical Christmas tree, and if you ask it for something you really, really, really want, and if you plant it in something cold enough, it'll grow into what you asked for.'

Barry blinked. '*Magic bean?* You've been living with that Trundle twerp for too long!'

Brenda just looked at him. Barry stared straight back.

'Do you think I'm an idiot, Brenda?' he said impatiently. 'There's no such thing as *magic*, and the North Pole is just a big pointless pile of snow. Now tell me the truth or I'll have this bean on toast for dinner!'

'No! You can't eat it!' Brenda yelped, jumping forward and flapping the instruction card in her dad's face.

'What the devil is that?' he said, snatching the card from her. He read it, trying to make sense of everything.

'Where did you say you got this from?' he asked slowly.

'The North Pole,' Brenda told him again. 'I'm not lying, Dad. Honest.'

Barry Payne might have been missing from her life for the past year – but he still knew his daughter.

'You're being serious, aren't you?' He stared at her, his eyes narrowed. 'I know when my own flesh and blood is telling porkies, and you're telling –' he paused and looked at the bean in his fingers – 'the truth?'

Brenda nodded.

'But – but what's the *point* in this stupid thing? Waiting for presents to grow in the freezer? It's just as bad as waiting for Santa to come down the ruddy chimney! Whatever it was that you were going to ask this bean for, one of my staff can bring you one from the toystore right away. Family rates, of course!' Barry winked.

'I wasn't going to ask for a *toy*!' Brenda blurted. She didn't mean to say it. It just came out!

'Well, what were you going to ask for?' Barry asked.

'Oh, nothing important. Just . . .'

Her father glared at her.

There was no escape. Brenda didn't know what to do. She was tired, and scared, and not thinking properly . . .

So she told him.

What Brenda Wanted

'Like I said, the bean came from a magical Christmas tree.' She sighed.

'And?'

'And you tell the tree what you want, and it sprouts these beans that you have to bury in the snow.'

'In the snow?'

'Yes, or in the freezer or somewhere else cold.'

'And then?'

'And then the beans grow roots in the ice and snow, and when the time is right they bloom toys, or whatever it is you wished for. That's how Santa gets the presents he delivers at Christmas,' Brenda explained.

Barry's mouth hung open like a fish. 'So you can ask for anything?' he said.

Brenda nodded.

'And this bean will give it to you?'

'If you're on the Nice List,' she said.

'And are you?' Barry asked.

'Am I what?' She pretended she didn't understand the question.

'Are you on the Nice List?' Barry repeated through his perfect gritted teeth.

Brenda nodded.

'Then it's obvious what you were going to ask for,' Barry scoffed.

'It is?' Brenda said.

'Of course. **MORE BEANS!** Why have one wish when you can wish for more wishes? It's the oldest trick in the book!' Barry grinned a greedy grin.

'No, you can't ask a bean to grow more beans. It doesn't work like that. You'd need a . . .' Brenda paused.

'A what?' Barry pressed, leaning in close.

She'd said too much.

The loophole.

The way to get more beans!

'I'm waiting. What would you need?' Barry snapped.

'You'd need your own magical Christmas tree . . .' Brenda said, trying not to cry. 'Just like Santa's!'

'Like the one that made *this* bean?' Barry realized, and Brenda nodded as tears began streaking down her cheeks.

The cogs in Barry Payne's head were reluctantly

turning. Thoughts were trying to get through with great difficulty – but eventually it all clicked into place.

'Now *that's* my girl!' Barry shouted, and stared greedily at the glistening bean in his hand. 'And all I have to do is ask it?'

Brenda replied with a slow, sad nod.

Barry held the bean out in front of him and cleared his throat.

'Listen up, bean, and listen good,' he barked.

'No, Dad! Don't do it! You're not on the –'

'Zip it, Brenda. You're not living with the Trundles now. This is my house, my rules, and whatever is under my roof belongs to me,' he snarled.

Barry stared hard at the egg-sized bean and narrowed his eyes.

'I want one of those trees she's talking about, that sprouts beans like you. A big one. A very big one. No, a

humongous

one that will sprout more magic beans than ever before!'

His voice echoed around the stainless-steel kitchen.

There was nothing Brenda could do to stop him, although there was no way that Barry was on the Nice List – so surely the bean wouldn't give him what he wanted . . . right?

Suddenly the red swirling pattern on the bean started to move and rearranged itself into the shape of a bow tied neatly on a Christmas present.

His request had been granted.

'Quickly, get this thing back in the freezer! Do whatever you have to do!' he ordered, carefully handing it back to Brenda as though it were the most precious thing on the planet.

With shaking hands, Brenda buried it at the back of the freezer in a small mound of frost.

'I'm sorry, William,' she whispered as she closed the door.

She couldn't help but think that if anything sprouted

WHAT BRENDA WANTED

out of that bean it was going to bring a sleighful of
trouble.

And she wasn't wrong.

CHAPTER SIXTEEN
GROWING TROUBLE

The second the freezer closed, Barry darted out of the kitchen, muttering to himself. Brenda followed him down the corridor to his office, only able to make out a few words.

'Growing . . . home . . . yourself . . . forget . . . Santa . . .' he babbled.

In his office, a disgustingly grand room of dark wood which smelt like the inside of a pencil case, he pulled out a leather-bound notepad and began to scribble.

'Dad?' Brenda said nervously, hardly daring to interrupt him.

He stopped abruptly.

'I've got it!' he announced, and suddenly leapt over his ornate desk. He flipped the notepad round so Brenda could see what he'd been scribbling.

'Grow Your Own Presents!'

he said triumphantly, as though it were some sort of magic spell.

Brenda blinked. Under the writing, he'd drawn what appeared to be a child pulling a BMX out of the freezer, with a big smile on their face.

'I – I don't understand,' Brenda said, although that wasn't exactly true. She thought she might know exactly what her dad was getting at, but hoped she was wrong.

'Pity you didn't inherit my intelligence . . . Allow me to explain,' he said, rolling up the sleeves of his shirt. 'First, we use the new magic tree that grows out of the bean in our freezer –' he flipped the page of his notepad to reveal a rough sketch of a Christmas tree – 'to grow thousands – no! **millions** – of new beans for us to sell to kids all around the world!'

He flipped the page again to reveal a sketch of

a small bean in its own little stripy packet that said

GROW
YOUR
OWN
PRESENT!

'What?!' Brenda gasped.

'I know – I'm a genius! GROW YOUR OWN PRESENT! If you want a bike? Ask your bean for a bike! Does your kid want a new telly? Plant your bean and watch it grow! We'll be shifting these by the bucketload and have zero manufacturing costs. All we need is that new tree you wished for. Whoever said money doesn't grow on trees! **PWAH-HA-HA!**' he quacked to himself like a greedy duck-witch.

'Dad, I –'

'I know what you're thinking,' Barry interrupted.

'You do?'

'Of course! You're thinking that I was planning on running off with the idea when that special bean in there belongs to you. Well, don't you worry, my little chip off the old block. I'm planning on cutting you in on the business,' Barry said, flashing Brenda his most disgustingly charming grin.

'No, Dad! That wasn't what I was thinking at all!' Brenda protested. 'That bean . . . well, it's special. I wasn't *meant* to ask for something to bring me more presents. That's not what Christmas is about.'

'Let me tell you what Christmas is about, Brenda. Christmas is about making money. That's it. All those catchy little songs on the radio, those teary adverts on the telly, those soppy books about family and belief . . . it's all to draw you in to SPEND! SPEND! SPEND!'

Brenda opened her mouth to speak, but Barry ploughed on.

'And do you know who makes nO money at Christmas?' he asked.

Brenda didn't have time to answer before Barry jumped in with, '*ME*, Brenda! Me! You'd think Mr P's Toystores would make a killing this time of year, but that Santa, he's got this season all wrapped up. I had a full shop today, totally rammed! Guess how many toys I sold?' he barked.

'**NONE**! Not one doll, not even a doll accessory, not a single blasted one. Do you know why? Because people visit Mr P's Toystores NOT to buy toys but to decide what they're going to ask Santa to bring. They see all the goods, but leave with nothing! Toyshops all around the world are just three-dimensional catalogues for that Santa clown. But all that's about to change, thanks to you!' He grinned, flashing his bleached-white teeth.

'But, Dad, I can't –' Brenda began.

'Of course you can. You're a Payne! You weren't meant for the Nice List. You're too much like your father!' Barry said, gesturing to a painting of himself riding an enormous black horse that was hanging above the fireplace.

'Oh!' Brenda gasped at the awful painting.

'It's a portrait, Brenda. I had it specially commissioned,' Barry explained proudly. 'All wealthy people have them, and one day you could have one too!

Why, with your little bean idea, you might just become half as successful as me! Partners?'

He held out his hand for her to shake. She stared at it for a moment.

'No!' she snapped. 'I don't want anything to do with this. That's MY present in the freezer, and you're not dragging it into one of your business deals!'

'Oh, I think it's a little late for that now . . .' Barry

shook his head, a disappointed expression on his smarmy face.

'What do you mean?' Brenda asked.

'Well, I'm afraid that what grows on my property IS my property. That bean belongs to me now. And, since you're the one who planted it there, you're already involved. In fact,' he went on, a nasty smile spreading across his face, 'you really should take all the credit for this, Brenda. It was all your idea! I wonder what your precious Santa would say if he knew what you'd done. Perhaps we should tell him?'

Brenda stared at him, horrified. 'No – please don't tell anyone!' she whispered. 'If Santa found out – and William . . .'

'Oh, don't worry, Brenda! I'll keep your little secret – so long as you don't try to stand in my way. Now then, let's try that again. Partners?'

He held his hand out once more.

There was nothing Brenda could do. She was an accomplice to her dad now – whether she liked it or not. She had no choice but to shake his hand.

'Partners,' she gulped.

CHAPTER SEVENTEEN
THE PUZZLE OF THE DANCING JINGLEWATTS

That night, Santa was awoken abruptly by a commotion in the North Pole. It was the sound of panicked elves in Elfville. There was crying and singing, screaming and singing, the faint thud of the more overdramatic elves passing out in the snow . . . and more singing. Add to that the sound of a roaring dinosaur and you have a right racket!

'What the jingle is going on?' Santa croaked as he climbed out of bed in his silky red pyjamas, slipped on his dressing gown and threw open the window.

As he looked down on Elfville, he saw elves frantically

throwing something gold and shiny around like a hot potato while screaming as though the object were cursed. The Christmasaurus leapt after the shiny thing as the elves tossed it around – it looked like some very strange game of dino-in-the-middle.

Santa bounded down through his Snow Ranch and trudged through the midnight snow to Elfville, where his most trusted eight elves – Snozzletrump, Specklehump, Sparklefoot, Sugarsnout, Spudcheeks, Starlump, Snowcrumb and Sprout – and the Christmasaurus greeted him with faces full of fear and worry.

THE PUZZLE OF THE DANCING JINGLEWATTS

'Santa! Santa! Come and see!
Things aren't as they're meant to be.
Just look at all the jinglewatts!
They're falling! Can you make them stop?'

they sang.

Santa looked down at the elves in the tiny streets below him and saw that the object the elves were throwing around was the brass beliefometer, the magical device that measured children's belief in jinglewatts.

'My goodness!' he gasped. 'This isn't good, not at all, especially this close to Christmas . . . Let me take a look!'

The elves handed the beliefometer to Santa, who held it up for a closer inspection. Right before his eyes, he saw the glowing red liquid inside drop down a notch on the jinglewatt scale.

'Now that can't be right,' he said, giving the magical measuring device a little tap.

Suddenly the jinglewatts jumped back up again.

'What is it, Santa? What's the reading?
How many jinglewatts are kids believing?'

asked Sprout, the wisest of the eight elves.

'Well, the jinglewatts seem to be jumping around all over the place tonight!' Santa looked puzzled as the red liquid dropped and then climbed, climbed then dropped . . . then dropped, then dropped and then climbed again.

'In all my years, I've never seen the jinglewatts behave like this! It's almost as though they're sensing a shift in the air, a change. It's like something big has happened,' Santa said as he thoughtfully scratched his beard.

'Something good? Something nice?' the elves asked hopefully.

'It's hard to tell, but we must monitor this closely. I feel a disturbance in the air tonight,' Santa said as a chill blew through Elfville, causing all the elves to huddle together.

The Christmasaurus nudged Santa's arm and let out a concerned roar.

'I'm sure William's absolutely fine,' Santa replied, and the Christmasaurus sighed in relief.

'To bed now, all of you.' Santa smiled. 'Try not to worry.'

THE PUZZLE OF THE DANCING JINGLEWATTS

'But, Santa, we can't rest a peep
Unless you sing us all to sleep . . .'

the elves said.

And so Santa spent the next hour tucking the elves into their tiny beds in their tiny houses before popping his large bottom down on the snow, with the Christmasaurus curled up next to him, as he sang them all a little lullaby. But butterflies of worry were flapping their wings deep inside his round belly as his mind tried to piece together the puzzle of the dancing jinglewatts and the disturbance of belief.

CHAPTER EIGHTEEN
DISTURBING BELIEF

That night, Barry Payne kept running to the kitchen, opening the freezer and checking to see if the new magical Christmas tree had grown.

'Why isn't the blasted thing working?' he barked in the early hours of the morning.

'We only planted it a few hours ago, Dad. I don't think it will be ready until Christmas.' Brenda yawned, having heard the footsteps pacing past her bedroom door and followed him.

'Christmas? **CHRISTMAS**?!' Barry exploded. 'Well, that's our plan up the chimney then, isn't it? We can't sell presents to people AFTER Christmas. This bean is about as useful as a pile of reindeer poop . . .'

Barry paused as though he'd been donked on the head with a very large Christmas pudding.

'*That's it!*' he exclaimed.

'What's it?'

'Poop!'

Brenda stared at him in confusion.

'Fertilizer, Brenda. Manure. It speeds up the growing process!' Barry explained, then snapped his fingers. Even though the sun wasn't even up yet, Mrs Buttersby hobbled into the room.

'Yes, sir?' she said, fumbling with her glasses with one hand and tying her apron with the other.

'Fetch the gardener, at once!' Barry ordered.

'But . . . but, sir, this is an apartment. You don't have a garden,' Mrs Buttersby said timidly.

'Don't make excuses – just get a gardener here now!' he snapped.

'Yes, sir. Right away, sir . . .' Mrs Buttersby hobbled out of the kitchen and, sure enough, twenty minutes later, in walked a tired-looking man carrying a large heavy-looking bag and wearing a toolbelt with pruning shears, a small hoe and a trowel protruding from the holsters.

'Mr Greene's the name! Does someone need a gardener?' He stopped and looked curiously at Mr Payne. ''Ang on a sec, ain't you that toy bloke off the telly? My little kid loves your adverts! *Who needs Santa any more?*' Mr Greene sang, making Brenda squirm at the lyrics to the jingle.

'Yes, yes, that's me. Wrote the jingle myself!' boasted Barry.

'Well, sir, anything you need, you just let me know. Mrs Buttersby said it was something urgent?' Mr Greene asked.

'Yes, it is! We need to grow this bean overnight,' Barry said, showing the man the mound of ice shavings in the corner of the freezer drawer.

'Overnight!' Mr Greene burst out laughing, but quickly stopped when he saw the look on Barry's face. 'Oh . . . you're serious? Right . . . I see . . . well . . . what sort of plant is it?' the gardener asked.

'Never you mind that. Just soak the thing in as much

manure, Miracle-Gro and plant food as you can get
your hands on, and if there isn't a budling by sunrise
you'll never prune another petal,' Barry hissed. 'And
one more thing. This plant needs to grow in the coldest,
iciest conditions possible.'

Mr Greene shook his head, puzzled. 'Ice, eh? This ain't
like no plant I've ever heard of! But if you're sure . . . Mrs
Buttersby, could I trouble you for some more ice?'

Mrs Buttersby disappeared as Mr Greene took off
his toolbelt. Then he unzipped his bag of horticultural
tricks and started pulling out packets, bottles, fertilizer
enhancers, artificial vitamin supplements, Miracle-
Manure . . . Mr Greene had everything a plant
might need.

He nodded as Mrs Buttersby came back into the
kitchen, dragging two large bags of ice.

'Perfect. Fill this plant pot with it, please,' Mr Greene
said.

Barry looked at Brenda. 'Well, you heard the man!
Make yourself useful for once!'

Brenda reluctantly followed his orders, an awful
sense of guilt tumbling around in her stomach, while

Mr Greene dug the frozen bean out of the frost in the freezer and pushed it deep into the ice-filled plant pot. He started pouring in glugs of his chemicals.

'Dad, I'm not sure that's going to be good for the bean,' Brenda said.

'Don't be ridiculous. This man's an expert – just look at his equipment,' he snapped back, handing another bottle of fertilizer to Mr Greene to pour into the pot.

Disturbing Belief

'Now we just need to give it a good stir,' Mr Greene said.

'Let the girl do the honours . . .' Barry gave a horrid smile, and the gardener handed Brenda his trowel.

Reluctantly, she mixed everything together while Barry ran to all the thermostats in the apartment and turned them down to freezing, making the flat as cold as possible.

'That'll do,' he said, pulling Brenda away from the freezing bucket as though he expected something magical to happen. But nothing did.

'Well?' he said.

'Well what?' Brenda replied.

'Why isn't it working? We've done everything you said, haven't we?' Barry asked.

Brenda sheepishly pulled out the little card of instructions that Santa had given her, and Barry snatched it out of her hands.

'Done that . . . Done this . . . Done, done . . . Hang on a tick, this says that we have to sing to it!' Barry said, pointing at the card. 'Well, I'm not singing to a plant, that's for sure.'

Barry marched over to a small touchscreen on the

kitchen worktop. He tapped it, and music burst out of speakers built into the ceiling.

'Aha! Here we go!' He smiled as he turned up the volume. A lady that was belting out a song in another language so loudly that her vibrato made Brenda's head wobble.

'Erm, I think it's meant to be Christmas songs!' she shouted over the noise.

'Well, I make the rules now, and this tree is getting a musical education,' Barry said, turning up the volume until Brenda had to cover her ears. 'It's called *opera*, Brenda. It's what all millionaires listen to!'

Suddenly the music stopped.

'Hey! Did I say you could turn that off?' Barry barked.

'I didn't!' Brenda said.

They both looked over to the kitchen worktop and saw that a gross, giant, rotten-looking green root had twisted its way out of the bucket of ice like a mouldy finger of mulch and smashed the touchscreen controlling the music.

Disturbing Belief

'I didn't expect it to look like that,' Brenda whispered.

'Me neither,' said Barry, with an awful greedy grin across his face. 'It's better!'

Brenda woke to the sun coming through the kitchen window in her father's luxurious penthouse, having spent the rest of the night asleep on the cold tiles.

'It's ready,' her father whispered, and she rubbed her eyes to see him sitting on the floor with his tie hanging loose around the collar of his now-creased shirt, staring at the thing that had grown from the bean.

Instead of the little magic tree that Brenda had wished for, the bean had turned into something else entirely.

It was a disgusting mutation of a Christmas tree. It looked as though it were slowly crawling out of the plant pot, its branches reaching out like tentacles across the kitchen. Instead of pine needles, it seemed to have thick, dark, spider-like green hairs all over it, and it smelt of Brussels sprouts . . . from last year!

'Brenda! We're going to be filthy stinking rich and there's absolutely nothing Santa can do about it!' Barry cackled. 'Now then, you listen here, *tree*. It's time to give us our magical beans.'

He wagged his finger at the creature he'd helped create.

The tree did nothing.

'That's not how it works, Dad,' said Brenda with a sigh.

'Well, how does it work?'

'You've got to *ask* it,' she said.

Barry dropped down to his knees and, with no shame at all, started to beg the tree.

'Tree, please, please, *PLEASE* – grant me lots and lots and LOTS of magical beans! As many magical beans as you can make. Beans for every toy imaginable . . . cars, planes, unicorns, trains . . .' He rattled off a seemingly endless list of toys and gifts while the monstrous tree sat . . . listening.

'Well?' Barry asked once he'd finished. 'Did it work?'

The tree remained lifeless.

'Did I do something wrong?'

'Well, Dad, the thing is . . .' Brenda started to say.

'Thing? What thing?'

'You have to truly want it. Honestly, deeply, truly,' Brenda explained.

'Are you telling me that this isn't going to work because you think I don't really HONESTLY, DEEPLY, TRULY *WANT* to put Santa out of business and make mountains of money? Perhaps you're not destined to be a businesswoman after all,' Barry scoffed – and, at that very moment, there was a loud

POP!

Something sprang from the tree and flew through the air. Barry reached out and caught it. It was a bean pod all right – but not like the ones from Santa's tree. This one was as yellow as a rotten egg with a deep green swirl.

Brenda looked at her dad, whose face had lit up with wonder.

He's as cruel and crooked as his horrid plan, she realized. *A Naughty Lister through and through. This bean is proof.*

POP!

Another bean pod sprouted.

249

'Here they come! Brenda, get ready to catch!'

Barry laughed as the tree started firing out nasty, rotten-looking bean pods left, right and centre. It was like being in a popcorn machine as the room started filling up with the little yellow pods.

'Christmas will never be the same again!' Barry said with a cackle, throwing the bean pods into the air in celebration.

CHAPTER NINETEEN
BEAN AND GONE!

'D ad! DAD!' William yelled from the kitchen.

'What on earth is the matter, Willypoos?' asked Bob, out of breath from the dash down the hallway to see what had happened.

'It's the bean! My Christmas bean!' William cried in a panic. 'I can't find it anywhere!'

'Oh, thank goodness.' Bob sighed in relief. 'I thought something serious had happened.'

'This *is* serious!' William protested. He wanted to say that without that bean he had no way to get more of Sub-Zero's time-travel potion to go back in time and see his mum again – but Santa had warned him not to tell his dad about his little adventure to the past, or how he'd bumped into the younger versions of his parents and himself as a baby. So he could hardly start moaning about not being able to do it again!

'I need to tell it what I want and plant it in the freezer! Where is it? I wish I . . .' William paused – at the mention of *wish*, his new, fluffy white pet wish wafted into the room.

'No, not you! You live here now. You can make yourself at home. I'm not wishing on you!' William told the wish, and the soft little fleck of fluff seemed to droop with disappointment.

'Have you checked underneath your wheelchair?' Bob suggested.

'Yes!' William said.

'Your bedroom?'

'Yes, Dad!'

'What about the clothes you wore to the North Pole? Have you checked the pockets?'

William paused.

'That's it! My other pyjamas – I put it in one of the pockets!' he remembered as Pamela entered the room with an empty washing basket.

'Are you looking for your pyjamas? They're washed and folded in your drawer.' She smiled.

William's face dropped.

'Washed?' he whispered.

'Oh dear,' Bob said.

'Yes, why? Oh, they're not dry-clean only, are they?' Pamela asked, looking worried.

'No, it's not that, Pam,' Bob said awkwardly. 'It's just that William left his Christmas bean in the pocket. The magical one, from Santa.'

'And now it'll be smushed to a pulp!' William said through the lump that had formed in his throat.

'But I checked the pockets.' Pamela frowned, trying to remember.

'Not to worry, Willypoos. I'm sure you can write a letter to Santa and ask him for whatever it was you wanted,' Bob suggested, trying to cheer William up.

'Oh yes, that's a good idea, Bob. See, nothing to worry about, William,' Pamela said.

BEAN AND GONE!

'**No!** I was saving my bean for something special. For someone . . . Oh, you wouldn't understand,' William said sulkily, and an awkward silence fell over the room.

'You could always use your wish,' Pamela suggested hopefully, and the fluffy ball perked up again, ready and waiting.

'You just don't get it, do you?' William snapped, and he left the kitchen on the verge of tears. He was going to head straight to his room, but as he passed the living room something on the TV grabbed his attention.

It was Brenda's dad, **Mr P!** It was one of his awful TV adverts, but this one was new. William moved closer to get a better look, and that's when he spotted it . . . the thing in Mr P's hand.

It was a large bean, about the size of an egg, and it looked just like the red-and-white bean Santa had given him – except that this one was green and yellow, like the evil twin of one of Santa's Christmas beans.

'Dad, I think you'd better see this!' William called, glancing back into the kitchen, where his dad and Pamela were talking in hushed voices.

'I'll be there in a minute, Willypoos,' Bob replied.

William quickly turned back to the TV.

'Are you sick of the same old presents, year after year?' Mr P said. 'Are you looking for something different? Something new? Something MAGICAL?'

He waved his hands mysteriously in front of the camera, and the shot dissolved to reveal a toyshop display table piled high with hundreds of stripy packets of green-and-yellow beans.

'Then look no further! Mr P has just what you need. This year, you can

GROW YOUR OWN PRESENT

using these magical beans, brought to you direct from the NORTH POLE!'

William's jaw dropped. Did he actually just hear that right?

Mr P's Toystores . . . selling Santa's magical Christmas beans? *This is definitely not good!* William thought to himself as a million questions raced through his head.

How has Mr P got his hands on a Christmas bean?

Why is it green and yellow?

OK, so that was just two questions, but they were important ones!

'**DAD!**' William yelled.

Bob and Pamela came running in this time.

'What is it?' Bob panted.

'Look!' William pointed.

'It's just one of Barry's awful TV ads.' Pamela rolled her eyes.

'No, listen!' William said, turning up the volume.

'These are one hundred per cent authentic Christmas beans that are filled with magic, straight from the North Pole itself. You want a magical Christmas? You NEED a magical Christmas bean! Does your kid want a bike?' Barry said as a little boy popped up on the screen.

'Yes please, Mr P!' he squeaked.

'Well, just ask your bean for one! Then place it in the freezer in your very own home, and your bike will pop into existence just in time for Christmas, exactly like the elves do it at the North Pole!' said Barry, grinning.

The boy then pretended to plant one of the beans in a fake freezer. He closed the door and there was a *ding*! like a microwave. He opened the freezer and a shiny new BMX practically fell out on top of him.

'William, just turn it off. Let's not let that man ruin our day!' suggested Bob.

'No, Dad! This is serious!' William said.

Bob chuckled. 'Willypoos, don't worry! Of course Barry Payne isn't selling real magical beans from the North Pole. The man doesn't even believe in Christmas! There's no way Santa would let those things slip into the hands of someone like him. I mean, Brenda didn't even get one!'

BRENDA . . .

BRENDA . . .

BRENDA!

Brenda's name echoed through William's mind . . .

BRENDA!

BEAN AND GONE!

William's mind flashed back to the way she had stared at his magical bean in the sleigh, the way her envious eyes had lingered on his pocket once they'd landed, and then the unusually tight hug she'd given him when they'd said goodbye.

His heart froze as though the Winter Witch had clasped her icy hand around it.

Brenda took my Christmas bean!

His frozen heart was thawed by a hot anger boiling through him that he'd never felt before. Just as he was about to tell his dad, William suddenly remembered what Brenda had said when they were in the back of the sleigh.

'Ugh! That bean is wasted on you. I had loads of brilliant ideas. I'd already decided what I was going to ask for . . . It was just a loophole.'

A loophole? William wondered. Like the kind of loophole that would allow you to grow more presents? But, how could she get more? To get MORE PRESENTS, you'd need MORE BEANS, and to get MORE BEANS you'd need . . .

William realized why Brenda had stolen his
Christmas bean: to get her very own magical
Christmas tree, just like Santa's!

Mr P's face filled the TV screen and
appeared to be looking straight at William.
'Who needs Santa when you can grow
your own presents at home?' he asked,
winking.

'Oh, Brenda ...' William sighed.
'What have you done?'

CHAPTER TWENTY
THE GIFT OF
THE YEAR

There was a sudden burst of noise from the street outside. William heard car doors slamming, engines starting, children shouting excitedly and parents saying things like, 'Hurry up!' and, 'They'll all sell out!'

William shot straight out of the front door to see the commotion for himself, closely followed by Bob and Pamela.

'What is it, William?' Bob cried.

Out in the street they saw their neighbours frantically de-icing their cars and fumbling to lock their front doors.

THE GIFT OF THE YEAR

Some even ran down the street, still in their dressing gowns and slippers.

'They've all lost their beans!' Bob said.

'No, I think they all *want* beans . . .' said William slowly.

'It's just another one of Barry's tricks!' said Pamela reassuringly. 'He can't have any real Christmas beans, William. Your dad's right!'

But what if it wasn't a trick? William couldn't help feeling sure that something bad had happened. Some sort of . . . disturbance.

'Hey, William!' called Yusuf as he passed William's house.

'Hi, Yusuf,' he replied.

'Have you seen those ads on TV? How awesome are those beans? I want one . . . like, SO bad! I'm going into town now to try and get one before they sell out! See ya!'

As Yusuf headed off, a thought popped into William's head. If Brenda *did* have something to do with these beans, then he needed to find out – and maybe she'd be at one of her dad's toystores.

'Can we go to Mr P's toyshop?' William asked.

Bob looked horrified.

'You want to go and get one of those . . . those . . . things?' he asked, scrunching up his face like he'd smelt a bad smell.

'Oh no!' William said quickly. 'I don't want to buy one, I promise! I just want to see them. You know, find out what all the fuss is about!' He felt his cheeks flush red as Bob and Pamela glanced at one another, looking worried. He didn't have the heart to tell them his theory – that Brenda was responsible for all this!

'Well, OK,' Bob said. 'I need to buy some more fairy lights anyway. There's a dark spot on the roof that keeps bugging me.'

'Great! I'll see you there!' William said, and whizzed off as fast as he could.

'Wait for us!' Bob and Pamela cried as they tried to keep up – but in his wheelchair William had the advantage. He sped down the road, round the corner, and darted towards the high street and the little row of shops where the crowds suddenly got denser. William could hardly see through the thick crush

of people who all seemed to be heading in the same direction.

'William!' a friendly voice called from the crowd.

'Izzy!' William replied, spotting another of his class-mates, who was out Christmas shopping with her parents. 'Why is it so busy?'

'Haven't you heard?' Izzy said. 'Mr P's Toystore is selling –'

'Christmas beans from the North Pole?' William finished, his heart sinking.

'Yeah! Are you trying to get one too? Looks like the whole school wants one!' she said.

'You mean this whole crowd is all for the beans?' he asked.

'Yeah! Crazy, isn't it?' she said with a smile.

'Izzy, I'm not sure we should be buying them. I don't think Santa would want this!' William said.

'What? I can't hear you, William! Have a merry Christmas!' she shouted through the legs of grown-ups as she was swept away with the crowd.

William moved forward with the now extremely excited shoppers.

The Gift of the Year

'I can't believe our toys will actually grow at home!' one of them said.

'These beans are taking over the world!' said another, who was checking the news on his phone. 'THIS YEAR'S NUMBER-ONE PRESENT – BEANS!' he read aloud, and turned his phone round to show everyone a photo of Brenda's slimy dad holding one of his weird, mutated beans.

At that moment, a news van screeched up outside the front of the store, and Piers Snoregan, the famous news reporter, leapt out, closely followed by his camera operator and a team of make-up artists. They set up a shot in front of Mr P's Toystore while the make-up crew caked Piers's face in bronze powder, which made him look like he'd just come back from an extremely sunny holiday.

'Are you rolling?' he asked, and the camera operator nodded.

Piers flashed a smile at the camera. 'Piers Snoregan here, reporting from the busiest shop in the world right now – *Mr P's Toystore*, the only place you can buy one of these *magic Christmas beans*, which are expected to become the number-one Christmas gift this year! I'm here today for an exclusive interview with the man himself. Ah, and here he comes now!' Piers added, pointing in the direction of the sudden cheers and camera flashes.

'Thank you! Thank you!' Barry grinned, flashing his pearly white teeth, which made some of the crowd swoon.

'Mr P, thank you for granting me this interview,' Piers Snoregan said, shaking his hand.

'It's my pleasure. I always have time for my fans,' Mr P replied, winking down the camera.

'How does it feel to be the brains behind the number-one Christmas present in the world?'

'Well, this has been a long time in the making,' Barry explained smoothly. 'I first conceived this present many moons ago, but a certain someone at the North Pole wanted to keep these beans a secret from the world.'

William gasped as he heard boos in the crowd at the mention of 'a certain someone'. *How are they all falling for this?* he thought.

'But I felt that this present was so special, it deserved to be in the hands of the people. The children deserved the chance to experience the magic of Christmas in their own home,' Barry went on.

People around him were nodding enthusiastically. Yet William knew this was all just an act, and that Mr P didn't even believe in the magic of Christmas!

'Well, you certainly have a knack for knowing what kids want, Mr P!' Piers Snoregan said with a laugh.

'Yes, Piers, I do!' Barry boasted. 'But I couldn't have done this without my new business partner and loving daughter, Brenda. Come out here, Brenda!'

Brenda was suddenly ushered through the crowd by Barry's burly security guards and shoved in front of the camera.

'Well, hello there, little girly. You must be vewy pwoud of your daddy?' Piers said in a baby voice.

William saw Brenda's hand tighten into a fist, and knew that she was trying very hard not to wallop Piers on his bright orange nose. Her dad gave her a little nudge, and leant down to hiss something in her ear. Brenda took a deep, shaky breath.

'Yes, Piers,' she answered robotically, as if reading from a script. 'I am over the moon about my dad being the best toy provider in the world. Merry Christmas, everyone, and don't forget: the only place you can get your very own Christmas bean is right here at Mr P's Toystore.' She looked down at her feet miserably as she finished.

'Ah, my little girl is too kind!' Barry said, and the crowd burst into rapturous applause.

'Well, congratulations to you both. Mr P and his daughter!' Piers said, and the crowd went wild as Barry and Brenda were ushered back inside the store.

THE GIFT OF THE YEAR

Piers turned back to the camera.

'Well, folks, it seems that it's the bloke behind the beans who's bringing joy to the world this year and, with so many children growing their own presents at home, it begs the question – do we really need Santa? This is Piers Snoregan signing off.'

CHAPTER TWENTY-ONE
INVISIBLE ELVES

POP!

'What in the jingle was that?' Santa said, lifting his head from the Nice List, which he was checking for the final time in the library of the Snow Ranch.

POP!

There it was again. The Christmasaurus heard it too as he woke up from his comfy snooze at Santa's feet.

The doors suddenly burst open and eight elves tumbled into the room.

INVISIBLE ELVES

'Snozzletrump? Specklehump? Sugarsnout? Sparklefoot? Snowcrumb? Spudcheeks? Starlump? Sprout?
What's going on?' Santa asked, closing the list and
jumping to his feet.

> 'Santa! Santa! Come and see!
> Things aren't as they're meant to be.
> We're not all there! We're not all here!
> We have begun to disappear!'

they sang in terrified harmony as they tripped over one
another in panic.

Santa held one large hand out in front of Sparklefoot.

'May I take a closer look?' he said calmly, and she
stepped on to his palm. He lifted the tiny elf closer to his
reading light and, to his astonishment, the light passed
right through her.

'Good King Wenceslas! You're right!' he whispered
in shock. He could see right through the elf. She was
becoming more and more transparent by the second.

She would soon disappear altogether!

273

'Santa! Can't you make this stop?
I feel as if I'm going to . . .'

POP!

Sparklefoot vanished. Her fellow elves gasped and the Christmasaurus whimpered with sadness.

'Now, now, let's remain calm. I'm sure there's a simple solution for all this,' Santa said quickly.

**'If the children on your list
Don't believe, we don't exist!'**

Sprout said, pointing with his partially invisible hand at the large, leather-bound Nice List that Santa had been reading.

'No, no, no! That can't be the case. It's almost Christmas! Belief will be soaring through the hearts and minds of children all around the world, dreaming of me and the reindeer –'

The Christmasaurus growled.

'And, in William Trundle's case, the Christmasaurus – flying across the sky with their presents! Here, I'll show you!' Santa said, reaching for the brass beliefometer that was sitting on his desk. He lowered it so the elves could see, and everyone huddled around the magical device.

There was silence for a moment as they all stared at the red liquid inside. Then, slowly, the red line began to fall down the jinglewatt scale. Further and further it dropped, all the way to the bottom.

'It can't be . . .' Santa whispered.

Suddenly there was another **POP!** This time it was Spudcheeks who had disappeared, leaving behind nothing but a half-eaten crumpet.

Then Sugarsnout – **POP!**

Specklehump – **POP!**

Starlump – **POP!**

Snowcrumb – **POP!**

Sprout – **POP!**

And last but not least, and with a final, nervous little bum-trump, Snozzletrump – **POP!**

Santa looked at the Christmasaurus, whose eyes were glistening with tears.

'Don't worry, my friend. We'll find a way to put this right,' Santa said shakily, and went to pat the dinosaur on his scaly head . . . but paused with his hand just a few centimetres away.

INVISIBLE ELVES

The Christmasaurus tilted his head inquisitively to see what was the matter. He saw a look of worry on Santa's warm face that he'd never seen before, and after staring at him for a few moments he realized why.

The Christmasaurus was looking *through* Santa's hand. He was becoming invisible too.

Santa was starting to disappear!

CHAPTER TWENTY-TWO
IT'S CHRISTMAS!

The days flew by in the final countdown to Christmas. Advent calendars were getting lighter as nearly all the chocolates they held had been eaten, and it was already the one night of the year when children all over the world were going to bed excitedly, without being asked to. It was Christmas Eve!

This year, though, instead of dreams of flying reindeer and Santa climbing down the chimney with a sackful of presents, children were dreaming of one thing.

The green-and-yellow bean in the freezer!

William woke up early on Christmas Day. The sun hadn't risen yet and the blue glow of moonlight lit up his room. He glanced at his dinosaur alarm clock: 5:30 a.m.

His heart skipped. Santa *MUST* have been by now!

But why hadn't the Christmasaurus woken him? He promised he'd say hello. William had even thought he might get a ride on the sleigh!

Since realizing that Brenda had taken his Christmas bean, dashing all his hopes of travelling back in time to see his mum again, the thought of spending some time with the Christmasaurus was the only thing that had kept William going through December.

So where was he?

He pushed away the dinosaur duvet, slipped on his warm dinosaur slippers and dressing gown, manoeuvred himself into his chair and silently went to the living room.

The soft twinkle of lights from the Christmas tree was enough for William to see that there were no presents under the tree yet.

The toasted crumpet, carrot, mince pie and glass of milk he'd put out for Santa last night were still on the plate by the fireplace, untouched.

That's odd, William thought. *He's running very late!*

'Aaaaaaaarrgh!'

A shriek from somewhere outside broke the early-morning silence.

What on earth is that? William thought, quickly heading to the front window. He glanced across the snow-covered road and realized that shouts and screams were coming from one of the houses opposite.

'WAAAAAH!'

Another cry came from another house, and William saw the living-room lights flickering on.

Gradually, the whole street was waking up and the shrieks, screams and cries of children filled the air.

'What's going on?' Bob called sleepily from the hallway.

'I don't know,' William called back. 'It's coming from the houses over there.'

It's Christmas!

'It's all the houses with children,' yawned Pamela, coming to stand next to William at the window.

She was right.

As soon as she'd said that, a front door opened and a man with a very cross face marched outside, carrying something very strange. It looked a little bit like a bike, but the wheels were oddly shaped and the tyres were sloppy and steaming, as though they were made of warm manure and fertilizer. The handlebars were the wrong way round and the whole thing was a disgusting yellow colour with evil green stripes. The neighbour threw the bike into the wheelie bin in the front garden, which rattled and shook as though the bike were some sort of living creature!

'Was that a bike?' Bob asked, joining them.

'I think it was meant to be . . .' William said slowly. Everything was beginning to click together in his mind.

'It's the same colour as . . .'

'BARRY'S BEANS!'

they all said at the same time.

At that very moment, another front door opened and a whole family ran out into the street, screaming as though they were being chased.

'What the jingle . . .?' Bob said, craning his neck to get a better look.

Suddenly a small army of toy soldiers marched out of the house and into the street, like zombies. Their eyes were glowing green as they began pulling up the winter flowers from the gardens that they passed and knocking the rubbish bins over.

'Oh dear . . . someone ought to take their batteries out,' Pamela said.

'Look, I think she's trying to!' Bob said, pointing to a woman in a dressing gown who was struggling with one of the wriggling toy soldiers. She finally managed to prise open the battery panel on the back, but . . .

'**It's empty!**' the woman screamed in disbelief as the soldier bit her finger and leapt to the ground.

William watched in silence. He already knew that these toys weren't being powered by batteries. They were running on magic . . .

dark magic!

Next, a huge green monster truck burst through a window, sending glass shattering out on to the street. William watched as it bounced up on top of the parked cars and drove over them, denting the metal and setting off their alarms.

'Something's gone very wrong!' Bob said.

'That's not all, Dad. Look under the tree!' William said.

Bob turned and almost fainted. Luckily, Pamela was there to catch him.

'Bobsicle, what is it?' she said worriedly.

'N-n-no presents? C-c-crumpet not eaten? S-S-Santa . . . S-S-Santa . . .'

he stuttered, unable to actually say the words.

'Santa hasn't been!' William said for him.

It was too much for Bob to bear – and he was too much for Pamela to carry, so she plonked him down on the sofa where he lay in shock. As he landed, he sat on the TV remote and the screen flickered on.

'Breaking news!' Piers Snoregan announced from behind the desk of his morning TV show. 'Christmas Day has got off to a bad start, with millions of children waking up to discover that the most popular present of the year – Mr P's magical beans – haven't worked. I repeat, THE BEANS HAVEN'T WORKED! We're getting reports of broken presents, faulty presents, and even presents attacking family members as they are removed from freezers around the globe.'

'This is unbelievable!' Bob mumbled.

'To make matters worse, early reports are suggesting that Santa did not make his annual chimney visit this year. And, because so many children were relying on the beans from Mr P to give them their Christmas gift, it appears that we might be facing a Christmas without . . . well, without *Christmas*!'

'But what happened to Santa?' Bob yelled at the TV.

'And what about Brenda?' gasped Pamela.

'I'm sure *she's* OK. She can take care of herself. It's what she does best,' William snapped.

'William,' Bob said, turning to his son and frowning. 'That wasn't very nice. None of this was Brenda's fault.'

Suddenly Piers Snoregan held his hand to his ear as though he were being told something very important.

'I'm being told something very important,' he said. *See!*

'We're about to go live to one of Mr P's Toystores where, I've been informed, Barry Payne himself will be making an official announcement.' Piers Snoregan cut to a live shot from outside the toyshop, where a crowd of angry parents had already gathered.

'Look, there he is!' Bob pointed at the TV as Barry appeared at the doors of his shop. The crowd rushed forward, shouting horrible things, holding up their broken toys and throwing snowballs.

'He's done for!' Bob said.

'Good!' Pamela said.

'Please, let me speak!' Barry shouted over the rabble.

It's Christmas!

The crowd slowly hushed and calmed enough for him to be heard. He pulled a little slip of paper out of his suit pocket and began to read.

'In the early hours of this morning, I started receiving messages of disappointment about our most popular item: the magic Christmas bean,' he began.

'*Disappointment?* The toy dog that grew out of my daughter's bean nearly ate our cat!' blasted an angry customer from the crowd.

'I take full responsibility for this. *However ...*' Barry said dramatically, folding up the piece of paper and looking directly down the camera and straight into the homes of the millions watching, 'I feel it is my duty to inform you that the faulty product can be traced all the way back to our supplier at the North Pole. **SANTA!**'

Barry shook his head in feigned disappointment. 'It is an absolute disgrace that the person we put our deepest belief in year after year has let our children down so badly.'

The angry crowd started mumbling to each other, absorbing the words spewing from his lying lips.

'Empty promises. No presents. Crying children. Santa

has gone too far this time!' Barry cried.

'He's right!' yelled a distraught father from the crowd.

'It's time for a change. It's time to show Santa that he can't do this any more,' Barry declared.

'**Yeah!**' agreed a small section of the crowd.

'It's time to put an end to these stupid, outdated traditions.'

'**Yeah!**' cried a slightly bigger portion of the crowd.

'I propose a future in which our children can have whatever they want, whenever they want it. None of this writing letters. None of this putting out mince pies and carrots. None of this waiting for a flamboyant fat fella to sneak down your chimney just once a year!' Barry cried, punching the air.

'**YEAH!**' the whole crowd now agreed.

'So here's to a future where your children can get presents from me, Mr Payne, all year round! Here's to a future with NO SANTA!' Barry took a breath and looked straight down the camera again.

'Here's to a future with . . . NO CHRISTMAS!'

The crowd went hysterical. The noise was deafening as Barry gave a triumphant nod at the camera and slipped back inside his shop.

Pamela sighed. 'I really hate that man.'

'Me too,' agreed Bob.

'Me three!' said William.

'But what I still don't understand is why Santa didn't come last night,' Bob said, his forehead creased with worry.

At that very moment, there was a thud on the roof, followed by the stomping of feet.

They all stared at the fireplace and Bob's face lit up. Little lumps of black soot suddenly fell out on to the floor as though someone were climbing down the chimney. Then came a great clatter and a crash, and a great cloud of black coal dust filled the room.

William, Bob and Pamela coughed as the soot settled, revealing a very frightened, very blue dinosaur in the fireplace.

'Christmasaurus!' cried William, and the sparkling dinosaur leapt out of the fireplace, hopping this way and that around the living room.

'Calm down, Chrissy! Calm down!' William said, holding his hands out, but the dinosaur was

panicked and started nudging William's wheelchair towards the front door.

'Dad, something's wrong,' William realized, and the Christmasaurus nodded frantically.

'Where's Santa?' Bob asked. The Christmasaurus dropped his head low.

'Oh my goodness! What can we do?' asked Pamela.

William noticed something tied around the dinosaur's neck. 'What's this?' he said, touching the small red velvet pouch. He opened it and turned it upside down, and a single candy cane slipped out on to his lap.

William held up the Cosmos-Converting Candy Cane in the light of the Christmas tree, where it glistened with a magic that could only have come from the North Pole.

'I think I've got to go,' William said.

'Go where?' asked Bob.

'Back to the North Pole!'

CHAPTER TWENTY-THREE
BACK TO THE NORTH POLE

William hitched his wheelchair up to the Christmasaurus, using one of Brenda's skipping ropes and some fairy lights that Bob had been desperately trying to squeeze on to the house. He could have ridden the Christmasaurus, but he'd need his wheelchair when they got to the North Pole, so this seemed like the best way. And flying in it had been fun before!

'Willypoos, wait! It's too dangerous. I'll go,' Bob said as he and Pamela came running out into the street.

'Dad, trust me – I know what I'm doing.' William

tried to sound confident, but the truth was that he had absolutely no clue what he was doing! Still, he knew he had to try.

'No, William. Not after last year,' Bob said firmly.

William sighed – then an idea popped into his head.

'Hey, Dad, one of the fairy lights on the roof has blown!' he said, pointing over his father's shoulder.

'What?! Where?' Bob gasped, and turned round.

'NOW, CHRISTMASAURUS!'

William cried, gripping the push rims of his wheelchair tightly. **'I believe in you!'**

The shimmering dinosaur was off in a blue flash, galloping down the street before Bob and Pamela could do anything about it. The fairy lights wrapped around his scaly body glowed with the power of William's belief as the ground gradually disappeared beneath the Christmasaurus's thundering claws.

William was worried about being spotted by the people below. Had anyone looked out of their window at that moment, they would have seen the most spectacular sight: a boy in his wheelchair being pulled

by a shimmering blue dinosaur, flying up and away from the snowy street and into the Christmas morning sun. But that was the least of William's concerns now.

The Christmasaurus galloped through the air, dancing in and out of clouds, sniffing for the scent of the North Pole.

William knew how incredible this moment was, but all he could think about was Santa. For him not to deliver presents on Christmas Eve – well, something terrible must have happened, and William needed to find out what!

'What's that?' he said, spotting a crowd gathered in the street below. The Christmasaurus circled down to get a better look and they saw that it was the crowd outside one of Mr P's Toystores. Now, though, instead of protesting against Mr P, they were protesting against Santa – and against Christmas itself! The voices rang out into the sky as they chanted to the tune of 'Jingle Bells':

'CHRISTMAS BAN!
CHRISTMAS BAN!
CHRISTMAS BAN TODAY!'

'*CHRISTMAS BAN?*' William gasped. That was exactly what he had seen when he'd visited the future. 'No way!' he whispered to himself.

He remembered what Santa had told him about time, and about how every tiny moment and decision would lead down a different path – a different frosticle. Had the frosticle of the future he'd seen already begun, that very morning, with Brenda, her dad, and the magical Christmas beans?

The Christmasaurus roared and nodded his scaly head at something below.

'That's Brenda!' William shouted, spotting the twirly blonde hair in the alley at the back of Mr P's Toystore.

The Christmasaurus started descending, but William yanked on the skipping rope. 'I'm not saying a single thing to that Christmas traitor!' he said, straining to pull the Christmasaurus away.

The Christmasaurus huffed through his nose, but William didn't want to listen to him.

'Yes, she *is* a traitor! This mess is all because of her.'

The dinosaur pulled against the makeshift reins again and flew down over the alleyway. William saw Brenda launching a fistful of snow at the **MR P** sign on the back of the shop. The Neverball she'd wished for in the North Pole splatted all over the sign, then magically re-formed itself and shot straight back to her hand.

She wiped her eyes with her sleeve. They were red and blotchy, as though she'd been crying for some time, and her lips were blue from the cold.

Clutched tightly in her other hand, William saw the

snow globe his dad had given her to remind her of home.

The Christmasaurus glanced back at William and blew a huff of steamy air out of his nostrils.

William sighed. He knew that the Christmasaurus was right, and it's never wise to argue with a dinosaur.

'OK, OK! If you insist!' he said, and reluctantly guided the Christmasaurus down to make a soft landing in the alley.

'Christmasaurus!' Brenda yelped at seeing them land unexpectedly in front of her. 'And WILLIAM! I'm *so* happy to see you!'

She ran over and hugged the Christmasaurus, and then opened her arms to William, but he turned his face away.

'I know . . . I don't know what to say,' Brenda said, tears instantly filling her already-wet eyes.

William said nothing. The Christmasaurus nudged him with his enormous glittering head.

William sighed. 'Fine! Brenda, you took it, didn't you? My Christmas bean?'

Brenda nodded, barely able to look him in the eye.

'I can't believe you would do that to me. We're meant to be family now,' William said, knowing that would make Brenda feel a hundred times more guilty than she already did.

'I was going to give it back to you, William, honestly I was, but –'

'But you thought you'd let your greedy, rotten, Christmas-hating dad have it instead?' William interrupted.

'I didn't *let* him have it! Just as I was about to find a way to get it back to you, he found it and –'

'And you told him what it was?'

Brenda nodded slowly.

'*And* how to use it?'

She nodded again and William sighed with disbelief.

'You don't know what he's like, William. He knows when you're not telling the truth!' she explained.

Silence fell over the three of them for a moment. Chants from the other side of the shop filled the air.

'Brenda, there's something you should know about the future,' William said.

'But Santa said we shouldn't know too much about it,' Brenda reminded him.

'I know, I know! But I don't think I've got any choice.' He took a deep breath. 'Brenda, when I was in the future, I saw a world where there was no Christmas!'

Brenda gasped.

'No Santa, no decorations, no presents. Nothing! A total –'

'*Christmas ban!*' she finished, realizing what William was saying. 'William, you don't think that what happened today might have . . .'

'Set off a chain reaction that leads to a total elimination of Christmas all around the world, forever and ever!' he exclaimed. 'And that's not all. I saw a building, the tallest in the whole city, and at the very top there was one enormous letter . . .' William wheeled himself over to the wall and wiped away the splattered snow, revealing the letter $\mathbf{P}$. 'We've got to do something,' he finished.

'No, *I've* got to do something! This is my fault. *I* have to put things right!' Brenda said.

'No way. You've done enough damage,' William told her, tightening his grip on the fairy lights and getting ready to fly again. Brenda grabbed his arm and pulled his face round so he had no choice but to look her in the eye.

'Now listen here, Willypoos. You're my brother now –'

'*Step*brother . . . sort of.'

'*Whatever!* We're family,' she said, waving the snow globe in his face. 'And, if there's one thing I've learnt from you and your dad, it's that family should stick together. Now I'm coming with you to put this mess right. Got it?'

The Christmasaurus made a noise that sounded a little like a laugh. William rolled his eyes.

'OK, OK! You can come with us,' he agreed. 'But you're not sitting on my lap the whole way to the North Pole!'

The Christmasaurus chirped and crouched low for Brenda to climb on to his back.

Back to the North Pole

'I can't believe I get to ride you!' she said as she stuffed the snow globe and her Neverball into her pockets and made herself comfortable on the Christmasaurus's scaly back. She used two of the icy spines of his mane for handles as he burst into a gallop along the alleyway, before leaping into the sky, carrying Brenda on his back and pulling William behind.

'To the North Pole – and fast!' William called out, and with that the Christmasaurus dipped his head, flattened his scales and flew north like a shooting star.

CHAPTER TWENTY-FOUR
SNOWHERE TO BE SEEN

The Christmasaurus soared over oceans and mountains faster than you could turn a page, and before William and Brenda knew it they were landing in the vast white emptiness of the North Pole.

Brenda climbed down from the Christmasaurus's back and William slid the Cosmos-Converting Candy Cane out of the red velvet pouch and took a bite.

'Here, have some of this,' he said, handing it to Brenda, who crunched down on the magic treat.

Lights began to glimmer against the snow, and suddenly the empty snowfields were transformed, just as they had been before. But where there had previously been a bustling city full of elves and reindeer, snow people and fairies, and all sorts of impossible creatures, there was now nothing but a ghost town.

For the first time ever, the North Pole was silent.

All was calm.
All was white.

'Where is everyone?' William asked, and the Christmasaurus whimpered like a worried dog.

Cautiously they made their way to the Snow Ranch, the Christmasaurus pulling William through the deeper snowdrifts. They wandered past familiar places, but the familiar faces had gone.

'It's like they've all disappeared!' Brenda said, her whispered voice catching on the wind and echoing around the deserted city.

As they approached the reindeer stables, William and Brenda saw Santa's grand sleigh through the open barn doors.

'Look! It's still full of toys!' Brenda said, spotting the sacks of presents at the back of the sleigh.

'But the reindeer have gone,' William said as the reins and harness came into view, lying abandoned on the snow.

Something shiny and golden glistened in the morning sun; it lay on the light sprinkling of snow at the entrance to the stables. It caught William's eye and he pulled on the fairy lights and steered the Christmasaurus over to get a closer look.

'Is that what I think it is?' asked Brenda.

'Santa's beliefometer!'

William said, leaning over the side of his chair and scooping it up. He held it close to inspect the jinglewatt measurement.

'Not a single jinglewatt!'

'What does that mean?' Brenda asked.

'It means that children were so busy believing in your dad's knock-off beans that they've stopped believing in Christmas,' William said, his voice trembling.

The three of them glanced around at the empty Snow Ranch.

'If children stop believing, then Santa, the elves and

all the creatures up here stop existing! Santa told me that without a jinglewatt of belief to keep Christmas alive, he'd fade into nothing. And that's just what's happened!' William said.

'This is all my fault! I should never have asked for another stupid magic tree to get more stupid presents! If I could go back in time, I'd ask for no more presents . . . ever!' Brenda said, pacing up and down in frustration.

'Brenda . . .' said William, a thought coming to him. 'What did you just say?'

'No presents ever again! More trouble than they're worth.'

'No, before that!' William stared at her. 'Brenda, you said, *If I could go back in time.*'

His mind was racing. 'There's only one person who can help us!' he said, and he knew, as her eyes widened, that Brenda understood.

'THE WINTER WITCH!'

they both yelled, and, without hesitating, they all charged towards the Forbid Den.

They reached the entrance to the holly-bush maze

and, with no time to feel frightened, the Christmasaurus shot into the air, pulling William up above the bushes. William grabbed Brenda in the nick of time as they flew over the frosted hedges, landing in the witch's secret frozen lair.

'**Oh no!**' William cried.

Brenda followed his gaze to the centre of the snowflake-shaped fountain, where the Winter Witch had once stood. But she had gone, just like the rest of them!

'**No!**' Brenda cried, running round the fountain as if the witch might be hiding on the other side. 'She *has* to be here! Don't you remember what that grumpy sprite said? *She's always around. Now, then, today, yesterday, tomorrow.* She's in every moment!' She stepped across the frozen pool of the fountain to the empty plinth in the centre where the witch should have been standing.

'Well, it looks like Sub-Zero was wrong. It's just us here, and I don't see any witch,' said William. 'She was our only chance to put things right.'

'There might be another way . . .' Brenda said, her eyes wide and staring at something.

'Is that . . . what I think it is?' gasped William as he followed her gaze to the frozen goblet dripping with icicles that was perched on the edge of the fountain.

'It's full of Sub-Zero's potion!' Brenda said. 'Remember? It's what the Winter Witch uses to freeze time.'

'I know,' William said. 'It's what I was going to ask my bean for, so I could go back and see –' He stopped and swallowed hard.

'Oh. I didn't realize,' Brenda said, looking uncomfortable.

'It's OK. I've got to use it for something more important now.'

William took a deep breath. He knew what he had to do. This wasn't about him bending the laws of time and space to see his mum. This was about the future happiness of millions and millions of children. About restoring belief, so that Christmas, and all who depend on it, could exist again.

'I've got to use this to save Christmas,' he said. 'It's

too important. The future is depending on us!'

'No, William, not you . . . **ME!**' Brenda argued.

'No chance!' he replied.

'This is all my fault and it's for me to put it right. I'm not watching you disappear into the swirling depths of some freaky pool of time again. I have to face the consequences of my actions!'

William looked at the frozen goblet of magical, swirling liquid.

Brenda did too.

In that split second William knew that whoever got their hands on it first was going to drink it and . . .

THWACK!

A perfectly thrown snowball smacked into his face with such accuracy and force that he and his wheelchair started to topple over backwards. It was Brenda's Neverball – never melts, never misses!

William's legs shot up in front of his face and he tried to grab on to something – *anything!* – to stop his fall. He fell on to his back, but managed to twist round just in time to see Brenda's hands lift the witch's frozen goblet!

'No, don't!' he shouted.

'I've got to, William. I've got to go back and stop myself stealing that stupid bean!' she cried, dashing over to the plinth.

'No, Brenda! There's another way!' William shouted – but it was too late.

Brenda put the goblet to her lips and began to pour all the glowing liquid into her mouth.

William held his breath as she keeled over, dropping the goblet and holding her head.

'Ow, ow, OW!
It's s-s-so . . .
COLD!'

she gasped, trembling, her lips already blue from the potion's magic – or was it a curse? She shook and shivered as the icy liquid took hold of her mind. 'It's l-l-like the

b-b-biggest b-b-b . . .

b-b-b-BRAIN
FREEZE
EVER!'

she said, somehow finding the strength to stand.

311

THE CHRISTMASAURUS AND THE WINTER WITCH

Huge clouds formed above the Forbid Den in a threatening, thunderous, bubbling brew of greys and deep blues, swirling in a whirlpool in the sky over the fountain.

'Brenda, don't! It's not safe!' William shouted, but it was too late. An icy thunderbolt smashed down from the sky, cracking open the frozen pool with such force that Brenda lost her balance. She wobbled atop the plinth, waving her arms helplessly until it was clear that, one way or another, she was going to fall.

She took a breath and shot a look at William, and in that moment he saw that she had changed. Her eyes were gleaming with the same sharp icy-blue glow that he had seen in the Winter Witch's eyes.

He stared in shock. The Winter Witch had mixed the potion with icy water from the fountain, but Brenda had drunk straight from the goblet – and now it was taking over and transforming her!

Brenda spread her arms wide and let the fall take her, and all William could do was watch as she plunged into the frozen pool where time flowed on forever.

CHAPTER TWENTY-FIVE
FOLLOWING BRENDA

The Christmasaurus nudged William's chair back upright and he shot straight over to the edge of the fountain and peered inside.

'Brenda!' he called, but there was no one there. From the outside, the marble fountain looked just as it had before, shaped like a snowflake with the water inside completely frozen. It was as if he'd just imagined an overly dramatic thunderbolt crack the ice and his best-friend-sort-of-stepsister fall into the depths of time!

'Christmasaurus, we have to find a way to help Brenda,' William said, panic rising in his throat.

Following Brenda

Suddenly something twitched inside his dressing-gown pocket.

'What on earth . . .' William frowned, and a glowing ball of fluff floated out into the cold air.

'Wish! What are you doing here?' he said, staring at the fluffy creature that had secretly stowed away and joined them for the adventure.

The wish flitted over to the fountain and twanged its wish-receptor. William stared at the cute speck of magic, which seemed to be staring back excitedly. He could see that it was desperately longing for him to put its wish-granting powers to use. A wish was a handy thing to have at a time like this! But . . .

'I . . . I can't do it!' William sighed.

The wish sank a little, its white glow dimming slightly.

'Don't take it personally. It's just that you're a living creature too. I couldn't bear it if anything happened to you! This mess is our fault, and I can't let you vanish into nothing so that we can put it right. There *has* to be another way,' William said, taking the wish carefully in his hands and tucking it away in the safety of his pocket.

The Christmasaurus closed his eyes, straining to think.

Thinking is definitely not a dinosaur's strong point, though, and after a few seconds the Christmasaurus was distracted by something else. **A smell.**

'What is it, Chrissy?' William asked.

The dinosaur's nostrils flared as he put his nose to the snowy ground and followed the scent round a lap of the fountain. Then he sat down and wagged his tail proudly.

'What have you found?' William asked hopefully, rushing straight over to see. Sure enough, at the dinosaur's feet, there *was* something sticking out of the soft snow.

'It's the Winter Witch's goblet!' William breathed. 'Brenda dropped it when she fell!'

Leaning in for a closer look, he saw that the goblet was mostly empty. Barely a sip of Sub-Zero's potion was left at the bottom, which swirled and glowed with delicious temptation.

'A sip might just be enough,' William said excitedly as he carefully lifted the icy goblet from the snow, which had cushioned its fall. 'Do you know what this means? We can follow Brenda back in time and stop her from stopping herself – and messing things up even more!'

The Christmasaurus growled in an *are you sure that's a good idea?* sort of way.

William thought for a moment. 'You're right,' he said, sighing. 'Two time-travellers trying to change a wrong doesn't make a right! If only Santa were here. He'd know what to do.'

The Christmasaurus sat up straight with an excited chirp.

'That's it!' William cried. 'Santa! We'll go back just ONE day, to Christmas Eve, and make sure Santa delivers his presents. That way children will still believe, Santa will still exist, and then HE can help us get Brenda back. He'll know what to do!'

The Christmasaurus roared and leapt to his feet. William took a deep breath and looked into the icy goblet, which glistened with sparkling frost . . . or was it magic? Suddenly the sip of potion swirling at the bottom wasn't quite as inviting now that he had no choice but to drink it . . .

The Christmasaurus growled, sensing William's hesitation.

'OK, OK! Don't rush me!' William said, then he counted himself down. 'One . . . two . . . three . . .'

He swallowed all that was left of the mysterious frozen slush and tucked the goblet safely in his dressing-gown pocket.

There might not have been much left, but the effect was instant. Even the thoughts in William's mind were coming to a standstill as the potion took hold of his brain. He shook and shivered and jerked and jolted, every muscle in his body wanting to fight the freeze. William just about managed to crack his eyes open a squint, and through his frozen eyelashes he saw that the world around them was still. Totally frozen. Snowflakes hung in the air. Time itself was no longer ticking. The potion had worked!

'Fly, Christmasaurus! FLY!'

he gasped, holding his pounding head as the Christmasaurus shot into the air, pulling William behind in a great loop before diving nose first into the witch's fountain.

The ice shattered upon impact and the dinosaur and his passenger plummeted into the mysterious world within.

As they soared over the multiple fractals of time that spiralled out like a giant snowflake, William tried guiding the Christmasaurus, but he could barely see. It was as though his eyes were ice cubes sticking to the inside of his eyelids.

Voices from the past echoed all around them . . .

'Who needs Santa any more!'

'What on earth is a jinglewatt?'

'Welcome to Elfville!'

The Christmasaurus flew onwards . . . or was it backwards? As they soared across time, they looked into these echoes from the past for any sign of yesterday.

'But it's Christmas Eve! If we can't fly, then we can't deliver the presents!' Santa warbled from directly ahead.

'That's it!' William yelled, and the Christmasaurus flattened his scales and shot forward.

FOLLOWING BRENDA

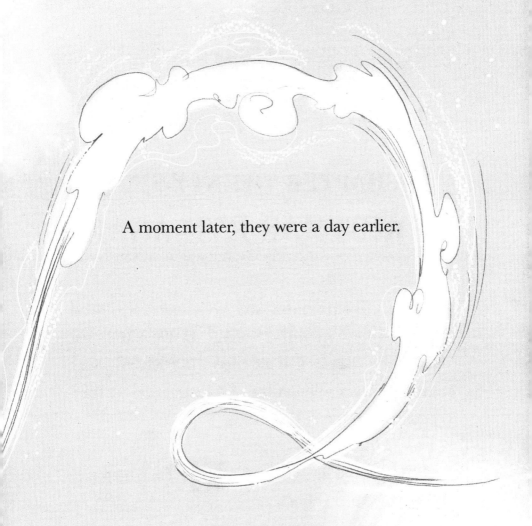

A moment later, they were a day earlier.

CHAPTER TWENTY-SIX
CHRISTMAS EVE AGAIN

The Christmasaurus and William crashed head first into yesterday, landing with a bump in a heavy snowdrift at the edge of Elfville. William's brain freeze was still numbing his thoughts as he tried to get his bearings.

'Did we make it?' he croaked.

The Christmasaurus roared – **YES!**

'Then we need to find . . .'

'SANTA! Only you can save us!

You're super-smart and so courageous!

Christmas Eve Again

**We will not panic or despair,
BUT GET YOUR SLEIGH UP IN THE AIR!'**

screamed a group of semi-transparent elves, racing past them.

'Follow those elves!' William said, still clutching his frozen head.

The Christmasaurus shot after them as they scurried towards the Snow Ranch. On the chase, William heard little whimpers of worry and fear from all around, accompanied by faint popping sounds.

POP!
POP!
POP!

He rubbed away the little clumps of frost that had formed in the corners of his eyes, like sleep, and through his eyelashes saw elf after elf pop right out of existence.

'We were right, Christmasaurus – there's not enough belief! Everyone's disappearing!' William said as they hurried to find Santa.

The vanishing elves desperately clung to each other, trying to stop their loved ones fading away, but William knew it was hopeless. After all, he'd just come from the future North Pole, and it was utterly *elfless*! Elf medics and nurses attended those mid-fade on the snowbanks at the side of the road, while fairies and wishes zoomed overhead, trying to escape – but, with the children of the world focusing all their belief on those rotten beans on Christmas Eve, the magical creatures were disappearing at an alarming rate. You just can't run away from a lack of belief.

'Final checks on the sleigh, and make it snappy!' Santa's bellowing voice boomed across the snow. The Christmasaurus raced towards it, dodging the frantic elf kerfuffle.

All of a sudden, the Christmasaurus skidded to a halt and William slammed into his scaly tail.

'**OW!** What is it?' he said, clutching his frozen and now-bruised head.

CHRISTMAS EVE AGAIN

The Christmasaurus whined and drew back low, as though he'd seen a ghost.

William followed his gaze and saw the Christmasaurus. Not *his* Christmasaurus. A second Christmasaurus!

The Christmasaurus too!

The Christmasaurus two!

It was the Christmasaurus of the past, from yesterday!

'It's OK!' William said, realizing that trying to explain time travel to a dinosaur was probably not going to be easy. 'He's just you on Christmas Eve.' He patted the Christmasaurus reassuringly as they watched yesterday's worried blue dinosaur help the elves secure the sleigh under Santa's watchful eye.

'We've only got one shot at this! We have to get these presents to the children no matter what or we're done for!' Santa shouted over the chaos, but it was too late. The elves taking his commands were

fading . . .

fading . . .

GONE!

'Reindeer, it's down to us now! We need to – Oh no!'
Santa looked at the empty harnesses at the front of his
sleigh where his Magnificently Magical Flying Reindeer
had been standing only a few moments before.

'We're too late,' he whispered, removing his gloves
and looking at his own transparent hands.

The Christmasaurus of the past leapt to Santa's
side, still glistening blue and not showing any signs of
disappearing.

'Christmasaurus, look at you! You're the only one
left! Yes, your William will believe in you forever.' Santa
smiled sadly and patted the Christmasaurus on his head.
Suddenly he gasped. 'Great crackers! That's it!' he
yelled. 'Christmasaurus, fly as fast as you can to William.
Tell him we need help! Bring him here, and let him see
what's happened. That boy is our only hope now!'

Yesterday's Christmasaurus immediately galloped
into the air above the deserted North Pole.
**'Fly! Fly with the wind in your
scales!'** Santa called after him as he soared away.

'Let's go!' William said to the Christmasaurus, who
was still a little shocked at seeing himself in the past.

CHRISTMAS EVE AGAIN

'Santa!' William called as they rushed over. 'We're here from tomorrow!'

Santa looked terribly puzzled, so William took a deep breath and explained as quickly as he could before Santa popped out of existence.

'The Christmasaurus came and found me on Christmas morning, but by the time we got here everyone had disappeared, then Brenda drank the Winter Witch's potion and now she's lost somewhere in time, trying to stop herself in the past from stealing my Christmas bean so that her rotten dad (*major* Naughty Lister!) can't ask for a magical Christmas tree like yours so that he won't be able to sell those magic beans to kids, which is what started off all this disappearing stuff, but luckily the Christmasaurus sniffed out the witch's goblet and I drank the very last drops in it and froze time so we could fly through it to yesterday, which is today, so I can help you deliver presents, and that way children will wake up and find their Christmas presents from Santa and believe in you again, and you'll still exist, and *then* you can help us get Brenda back!' William slumped in his chair with an exhausted sigh.

'I'm sorry, William, but I'm afraid my ears have already disappeared and I didn't catch a word of that,' Santa said apologetically.

The rate at which Santa was fading had rapidly accelerated during William's long explanation of the plot, and he was suddenly quite difficult to see.

'Santa?' William gasped.

CHRISTMAS EVE AGAIN

'Oh dear, William, it appears that I'm disappearing,' Santa said as his red velvet coat became as clear as ice. 'Before I go, I must warn you about freezing your mind again. It's not safe, William. The consequences can be disastrous for a human, especially a child. Just see what it did to the Winter Witch! I'm so sorry. I never wanted any of this to happen. But it was the only way . . .'

'The only way what?' William asked desperately as Santa tried to reach out his hand, but it was just a wisp of mist against the white snow.

And then it was gone.

There was a gentle thud, and William looked down to see Santa's beliefometer glistening in the snow. It was all that was left. The Christmasaurus bent down to pick it up in his teeth.

'No, leave it there! I'll pick it up when we come back here tomorrow, remember!' William said, showing the Christmasaurus the exact same one in his dressing-gown pocket. 'Now what?'

The Christmasaurus shrugged in a *how am I supposed to know, I'm a dinosaur* sort of way, before resting his scaly head on the dazzling red sleigh parked in front of them.

THE CHRISTMASAURUS AND THE WINTER WITCH

'That's it!' William cried. 'We have to deliver the presents. Me and you!'

The Christmasaurus jumped to attention. He was ready for action! Then he turned his scaly head towards the line of empty harnesses that lay lifeless on the snow, where the reindeer should have been, and he gulped nervously. There were no reindeer to help him pull the sleigh, and no Santa to steer it. The Christmasaurus was going to have to do this on his own.

'I know this isn't going to be easy, but I know you can do it, Christmasaurus! I believe in you,' William told his friend, and the Christmasaurus lifted his head and shook away his doubt.

'There's just one thing we need,' William added, and he pulled the Winter Witch's ice-encrusted goblet from his pocket. It was Christmas Eve. Time was ticking, and there was only one way to stop it. They needed to freeze time for a little longer, and to do that . . .

'Quick, we need to get to the kitchen!' William said, and the Christmasaurus licked his lips hungrily. 'No, not for food! We need more of the Winter Witch's potion!'

The Christmasaurus sprang into action, pulling

CHRISTMAS EVE AGAIN

William over a bridge out of Elfville that crossed a flowing river of warm mince-pie filling, through a candy cave, past the library and the cinema, down the toboggan run, and into the Snow Ranch. He didn't stop until they were in the deserted kitchen.

It was eerie without the hustle and bustle of busy elves roasting potatoes and buttering crumpets, but William had no time to worry about feeling scared.

He yanked open the freezer and stared into the harsh white light.

'**Look!**' He pointed at a small glass container between the ice-pops and fish fingers. 'It's Sub-Zero's coldron!'

The Christmasaurus peered in too and saw the freezing flames of erif, which were still ablaze, as though the grumpy little sprite had vanished halfway through brewing a batch of brain-freeze broth.

'That doesn't look right, though,' William said, leaning in to look at the black bubbling liquid inside the coldron. 'I don't think he finished it!'

The Christmasaurus roared in panic. They needed to freeze time again, and quickly. They weren't going to get another shot at this!

'What were the ingredients?' William searched his brain and tried to hear Sub-Zero in his memory . . .

A dash of lemon sorbet, a splodge of raspberry ripple and, finally, the secret ingredient that makes it colder than any other liquid in the world . . .

'A few shards of North Pole ice!'

William cheered, making the Christmasaurus jump. 'We need ice, from outside! **Go!**'

The Christmasaurus dashed out of the door in a flash of brilliant blue and was back in a matter of seconds with a mouth full of icicles.

'Perfect!' William said as he crushed them up and dropped them into the bubbling mixture.

The liquid came to life instantly, transforming into a bright, swirling blue. William picked up the coldron and poured the newly brewed potion into the Winter Witch's frozen goblet, ready to drink.

'Right then, let's get back to the sleigh,' he said, and the Christmasaurus took the skipping-rope reins in his mouth and pulled William all the way back to the wondrous vehicle.

William stopped next to the glimmering golden runners of the sleigh and hurried up the ramp. The Christmasaurus removed the empty reindeer harnesses with his teeth, leaving just one for himself, which he slipped over his head.

Without any hesitation, William lifted the icy goblet to his lips, but before he could drink any of the potion the Christmasaurus let out a huge

RooooAAAAR!!!!

William almost spilled the potion all over himself.

'What is it?!' he asked.

The Christmasaurus stomped his feet and growled at the potion. William knew at once what he was saying.

FAR TOO DANGEROUS FOR A CHILD!

'I heard what Santa said. I know it's dangerous for me, but we have no choice now,' William replied.

The Christmasaurus growled again.

'You? *You* drink the potion?' William repeated, and the Christmasaurus nodded his head confidently and opened his big mouth for William to pour the magical brain-freeze-inducing potion in.

William thought about it for a moment. Santa had explained that the potion was dangerous for humans, and especially for children – but he hadn't said anything about dinosaurs. And the Christmasaurus had been frozen in the North Pole ice for millions of years before his egg was discovered by the elves. If anyone could cope with a brain freeze, it was him!

William quickly tipped the potion into the open mouth of his scaly friend, who gulped it down.

'Well, anything?' William asked, waiting for the magic to take effect as he stuffed the empty frozen goblet back into his dressing-gown pocket.

The Christmasaurus shook his head. **Nothing!**

'OK, OK, keep your scales on! It might take a bit longer to work on dinosaurs,' William replied.

All of a sudden, the Christmasaurus's blue eyes widened. He shivered and shook and stretched his scaly back as the potion took control.

Christmas Eve Again

'It's working! Just let it freeze your mind!' William called out as the dinosaur squinted and squirmed as though his whole head were freezing. Then his mane of ice shards started to do something William had never seen before.

It glowed.

William saw that his magnificent, impossible dinosaur friend had transformed into something even more magical. Instead of shimmering, he was now glowing a bright icy blue from his pointy scales to the tip of his tail.

'**Whoa!**' William said. 'This is awesome!'

The Christmasaurus looked at his body and let out an excited roar.

'And look!' William cried, pointing to the sky overhead.

During the brain-freeze transformation, the night around them had frozen too. Snowflakes hung motionless in the air and not a single sound could be heard around them.

Time was frozen.

William glanced back at the impossibly large

sacks of presents in the sleigh, all squished in with inexplicable magic (the best kind!).

'Now what?' William called to the Christmasaurus. 'I've never flown this before!'

The Christmasaurus gave a roar, and William turned to the seat next to him. There he found Santa's gramophone with his favourite record already in place. He quickly fumbled with the needle, trying to get it to sit in the groove.

'Silly fiddly old thing! No wonder these became extinct!' he said. The little needle finally fell into place and cheery Christmas music filled the air.

'Got it!' William cried, and he felt the sleigh bob on the notes.

The dinosaur took a deep, chilled breath, and as William picked up the reins he started to move.

'Faster, Christmasaurus, faster!' William cried, and the Christmasaurus dug his illuminated claws into the snow and ran. He trotted at first as he built up momentum, then he cantered, and before he knew it he was galloping along, dragging the sleigh along above the tiny streets of Elfville.

'Whooooa!'

William screamed as the sleigh whipped through the air, scarily close to the fragile, elf-made buildings of snow.

Stormy weather was bubbling in the frozen sky overhead. The swirling winds of time were blowing in as the Christmasaurus leapt on to the toboggan run, with the sleigh hot on his scaly heels.

They plummeted down the first drop, giving the sleigh an injection of speed. William gripped the reins tightly as they zoomed round the loop and the sleigh shot towards the end of the ramp.

'I believe in yooooOOOOU!'

yelled William as his glowing dinosaur companion rocketed into the sky, faster than William had ever seen him fly before.

CHAPTER TWENTY-SEVEN
FUTURE
SUPER-SCROOGE

William and the Christmasaurus sped across the sky like a blue shooting star while the sleeping world below was kept in a frozen dream.

Suddenly the snowflakes that hung motionless in the air around them started to flash red.

Red snowflakes? That's weird, William thought to himself. He leant out of the sleigh slightly to get a closer look and realized that the snowflakes were reflecting the red of the sleigh, which had lit up like a giant fairy light on a Christmas tree.

'Why is the sleigh glowing red?' William shouted, and

the Christmasaurus roared down at the rooftops below.

Children!

William realized that the sleigh was telling him there were children below waiting for presents!

'Down there!' William pointed at the town beneath them, and the Christmasaurus spiralled down to the waiting rooftops.

'I believe you can land. I believe you can land. I believe you can land,' William repeated nervously as they raced through a forest of chimneys that shot past worryingly close to them.

The Christmasaurus spotted a nice clear rooftop ahead and pointed his nose at it while William clung on for dear life! Their first landing was a little bumpy, which was to be expected, and yes, they took out the TV aerial, the telephone line, the roof tiles of the two neighbouring properties and a Sky dish, but, as it was all just repeats at that time of year, William didn't think anyone would mind. What matters is that they landed!

'Now what?' William asked.

The dazzling dinosaur slipped out of his harness and ran back to the sleigh to help. He pulled open the enormous sacks, revealing seemingly infinite piles of toys. William saw that one present was glowing a subtle red, just like the sleigh. He pulled it out.

'So this must be the one for the kid who lives here,' he said as he handed it to the Christmasaurus, who carefully took it by the ribbon with his teeth.

'But how are we going to get this down the chimney?' William said, already feeling defeated by the task.

FUTURE SUPER-SCROOGE

The Christmasaurus looked at the skinny chimney, then back at William. They'd both seen Santa magically expand the world around him so that he could slip into people's houses with no problem at all.

'Without Santa, I've got no chance! Unless . . .'

The Christmasaurus perked up his scales, ready to listen to William's idea.

'Unless we do things a bit differently. I mean, what matters is that kids *get* their presents, not *where* they get them! Right?'

The Christmasaurus roared and nodded, jingling his gleaming icy scales.

'Christmas is about people coming together, so we should put the presents somewhere new, somewhere where everyone will find them *together*!' William said, and the Christmasaurus nodded. 'The front doorstep!'

The dinosaur wagged his sparkling scaly tail excitedly and leapt off the rooftop immediately. He was back in a flash with a huge grin on his face.

William suddenly felt something warm in his dressing-gown pocket. He reached in and fumbled around. It wasn't the icy goblet or even his wish that was radiating heat. It was Santa's beliefometer! It was as toasty as a cup of hot chocolate in his fingers as he pulled it out.

'Look!' William gasped at seeing the little red line rise up a notch on the jinglewatt scale.

'It worked! Delivering that present just changed the future. On Christmas morning, when Mr Payne's horrible beans go wrong, this present will be waiting for the child who lives here. The beliefometer is proof that, somewhere out there, this kid still believes in Christmas!' he said, full of proud excitement.

Overhead a clap of thunder boomed through the infinite storm of time, followed by a deep crack, like the first fracture in a frozen lake.

'One present delivered. We'd better get a move on!' William said. 'Do you think we can deliver them on doorsteps like that without landing?'

The Christmasaurus raised his frozen head towards the sky and howled a roar that lit up his icicles. A few moments later, they were airborne once again, and William was armed with an open sack of toys that glowed red as they approached their desired destinations.

The Christmasaurus swooped low and flew over the front gardens and driveways, the golden skis of the sleigh barely skimming cars and hedges!

'Michael Maxwell!' William read from the tag before dropping the luminous present perfectly on the doorstep below. 'Gemma Grosart, Chandra Chaudhary . . .'

Swish! Plop! Bonk!

The presents landed outside the entrances of houses and flats up and down the streets, lining them with beautiful glowing red boxes and making the beliefometer buzz with warmth.

After ten streets of doorstep present drops, William had really got the hang of it and was throwing them out like a basketball pro.

'This might just work!' he said, shoving his hands back in the sack for the next present.

'Hey, there aren't any more glowing presents!' he called. As he pulled his hands out of the sack, he realized the sleigh had changed too. It was no longer pulsing red – it was glowing green! A beautiful, glistening shade of Christmas-tree green.

Future Super-Scrooge

'Next town!' William cried, realizing that the sleigh was telling him there weren't any more presents for this town, and with that the Christmasaurus shot straight up into the sky and on to the next stop.

The moment the sleigh began to emit a deep scarlet again, they dropped down to the street, where William dished out the presents from his spot on the sleigh before whizzing off into the frozen night again.

William and the Christmasaurus covered towns and cities in no time at all, which was exactly where they were. Zooming across oceans with no waves, forests with no wind, as the sleigh flashed red and green behind the frosty blue hue of the Christmasaurus, it was all so beautifully magical that William had to keep reminding

himself that the very future of Christmas depended on them!

As the street lights of a small city approached and the sleigh began to radiate red once again, William noticed something.

'Christmasaurus, is it snowing?' he called.

The Christmasaurus slowed down a little and a snowflake drifted down past his nose.

William gasped. Time was beginning to unfreeze!

The snowflakes weren't falling at their normal speed; they were moving very slowly, as though time were just starting to think about ticking again.

'Your brain freeze! Don't lose it!' William shouted, and the Christmasaurus roared back. The dinosaur took long, deep sniffs of the freezing December air, and each time he inhaled his scales glowed brighter and brighter.

'That's working! Keep going!' William shouted as the Christmasaurus jump-started his brain freeze. In an instant, blue sparks of frozen electricity zapped down the Christmasaurus's spiny scales as the freeze took hold of his mind again.

The sleigh jolted forward as though the dinosaur

had been recharged with a burst of energy. William gripped the golden handrail of the sleigh, but had to let go instantly!

'Ow!' he said, looking at the icy burn on his palm. The metal handrail was well below freezing. William couldn't imagine how the Christmasaurus was coping with such a powerful brain freeze.

Worry leapt around William's stomach and two questions popped into his head.

Was this how it started for the Winter Witch?

If this is happening to the Christmasaurus, what on earth must Brenda be going through?

The sleigh suddenly lit up the static snowflakes in that glorious red again. They circled cities, cruised continents, crossed countries. With time on their side, they were an unstoppable force of Christmas spirit, and William felt the beliefometer practically jumping around in his pocket with the future jinglewattage rising rapidly.

William looked into the last sack of presents, which was now nearly empty.

'I think there's only one more town to go!' he shouted

to the Christmasaurus as the magnificent sleigh lit up for the final time.

'Down we *goooooooo!*'

William cried as the Christmasaurus swooped down for the next present drop, but before they reached the houses the clouds overhead split, revealing the swirling time storm.

'What's that?' William cried, pointing into the whirl-pool of moments that could be seen through the opening.

A series of lightning bolts streaked across the sky, and in their intense light William could see . . .

FLASH!

An enormous headquarters with a gleaming sign over the top that read **PAYNE TOYS**.

Thick black clouds pumping out of a polluting power
plant with two large letters on the two largest chimneys:
PP and underneath **PAYNE POWER**.

A huge building with a sign that read:
PAYNE ENTERTAINMENT.

An aeroplane flying overhead with
PAYNE AIRLINES on its tail.

A roller-coaster full of screaming children in a theme park called: **WORLD OF PAYNE.**

PAYNE PUBLISHING.

PRESIDENT PAYNE.

LORD PAYNE.

KING PAYNE.

BARRY PAYNE: THE MOST POWERFUL PERSON IN THE ENTIRE WORLD!

'NO!' William gasped, realizing these were flashes into the future. A future in which Barry Payne would still become the all-powerful, Christmas-banning future super-Scrooge!

'We need to keep going!' William cried to the Christmasaurus. 'We have to deliver them ALL! We need every child to believe. It's the only way!'

But, just as they were about to fly on, a burst of mysterious icy blue caught their eye. It was a person soaring across the flashes of the future, diving into one, then appearing in another as though they were in all moments of time simultaneously.

William suddenly remembered what Brenda had said.

She's always around. Now, then, today, yesterday, tomorrow. She's in every moment!

The Winter Witch! William thought – but then he heard a familiar voice . . .

'What have you done, Dad?'

Brenda! And she was somewhere in the future! William searched the visions in the clouds and, at last, found her face. It was Brenda . . . but she had changed. It wasn't just her eyes that had an icy-blue glow. Her

skin was pale blue and shimmering with frost.

'Brenda?' William shouted, but she leapt from one moment into another, crossing from one frosticle of time to another, causing another deep, icy crack.

'Christmasaurus, she's been jumping across the snowflake of time! She's trying to go back and change what she did! We have to stop her – it's too dangerous!' William cried. 'Santa said that time is like a snowflake made of different frosticles, and moving across them is what made the Winter Witch the way she is. We can't let that happen to Brenda!'

The Christmasaurus roared in agreement, instantly launching skyward in a vertical climb, pulling William and the sleigh up into the clouds. The glowing dinosaur pulled as hard as he could as the blizzard fought against the sleigh. It swayed violently from side to side like a kite in a hurricane, but they wouldn't give up. They had to save Brenda.

'I c-c-can't see anything!' shouted William. It was a total white-out, but voices boomed all around them.

'Who needs Santa!' Barry Payne spat from the future. 'No more Christmas EVER AGAIN!'

Then, in the blue light from the Christmasaurus's scales, William saw her again.

'Brenda!' he called out as they shot past her frozen figure, lost in a moment.

William was about to pull on the reins to circle back for her, but the Christmasaurus let out a roar as Brenda was suddenly ahead of them again, frozen in another moment.

'Brenda! You have to stop!' William screamed as the storm carried them along, but she was already in the past.

FUTURE SUPER-SCROOGE

Before he could get the Christmasaurus to turn round, a huge gust of wind slammed against the side of the sleigh, sending it into a spin.

'Whoa!' William cried, tightening his seat belt to stop himself falling out as the sleigh twisted upside down.

The storm dragged them this way and that. Ice and snow battered William and the Christmasaurus as they were pulled into the spin.

The force was too much for the Christmasaurus – even all eight reindeer would have been overpowered by the winds of time.

'I can't hold on much longer!' William cried out as they spun.

The Christmasaurus slipped his head out of the harness and turned to William, ditching the sleigh to save his friend before they were blown apart, but before he could reach William a great gust threw them out of the storm . . .

The sleigh crash-landed in a quiet, snowy street. Its skis slammed down on the tarmac with a spray of sparks, causing William to lose his grip. He was thrown out, and he hurtled through the air. While he went one way, the sleigh and the Christmasaurus went the other, and he hit the ground hard. His seat belt popped open and he toppled out, on to the cold, snow-covered pavement. His wheelchair landed on its side, just missing his head, and suddenly everything was still.

'Ouch . . .' groaned William.

Luckily, the layer of snow had cushioned his fall a little, but falling from an out-of-control sleigh while travelling through a time storm is always going to hurt!

He took a moment to recover, then tried to pull his wheelchair upright, but his frozen fingers slipped and he fell again.

'Oh my goodness! Let me help you,' said a friendly female voice from above him. The woman lifted up his wheelchair first and brushed the snow off the seat, then bent down to help William into it. He slumped down, feeling embarrassed and defeated.

'There . . . all better. Are you OK?' the woman asked, smiling.

William looked up and his heart stopped.

Not because time had frozen again. But because he was looking at his mum.

CHAPTER TWENTY-EIGHT
FOREVER FROZEN

'Are you OK?' William's mum asked him.

William was too stunned to say anything.

'You must have had quite a fall. What are you doing out this late on your own?' she went on.

'I-I-I was . . .'

The words just didn't come out. William stopped trying to say anything and instead just stared at his mother. Her eyes were brown, like his, and her hair was shorter than in a lot of the photos he'd seen of her, but he liked it. She wore a smart coat, and sparkly shoes that William thought looked like the sort you'd wear to a party.

'Are you being quiet because I'm a *stranger* and you're not supposed to talk to them? Well, that makes sense and it's smart. I'm Molly,' said his mum, and she stuck out her hand. As William made to put his trembling hand out to shake hers, she snatched it away and blew a raspberry.

It was childish, but its unexpectedness made William give a genuine laugh.

'That's better!' Molly smiled. 'Now you know my name, so I'm not a stranger. Let me take you home. Do you live around here?'

William hadn't even noticed where he'd landed when they fell out of time. They were a few streets away from their own wonky little house – except this was the past, and William remembered that his mum and dad hadn't moved into that house until after they were married. He thought, judging by how young his mum looked right now, that their wonky little house probably wasn't theirs yet!

He started to say no, but for some reason it came out as: 'Yes! I live a few streets away.'

'Then lead the way. Let's get you home.' She smiled and stepped aside for William to go first.

'What date is it?' he asked, trying to find out which year he'd fallen into.

'The date?' Molly said, laughing. 'You must know what the date is!'

William didn't.

'Well, it's Christmas Eve! The big night! That's why you should be home, getting ready for a little visit, if you

364

know what I mean.' She winked. 'That's if you've been good. You *have* been good, right?'

'I've made a few mistakes, but I'm trying to make up for them tonight,' he said.

'Well, there's always enough time for righting wrongs.'

They fell silent as they carried on down the street. William tried to think of something else to say. 'I, er, like your shoes,' he said shyly.

'Thanks! I'm on my way to a date. A first date actually!' said Molly, smiling.

'On Christmas Eve?' William asked.

'Yeah! And he's totally nuts about Christmas, so I'm surprising him with this.'

She reached into her pocket and pulled out a beautiful snow globe.

William's heart was racing. He recognized it instantly. It had a cosy hand-carved, little log cabin inside. It was the one his dad got out every Christmas.

William's mum had given it to his dad on their very first date – and Bob had kept it all these years!

Then his heart raced even more: his mum was on her way to meet his dad right now!

'I made it myself. Do you think he'll like it?'

'He'll love it.' William smiled, then suddenly realized that must sound really odd. How could he possibly know what the boyfriend of a total stranger he'd only just met would like? 'I mean . . . I would like that, if I were him.'

Tucking the snow globe back into her pocket, Molly glanced at William suspiciously for a moment, then chuckled as they came to the corner of the street.

The evening was magical. Stars overhead twinkled in the crisp, Christmas Eve sky. The houses looked warm and inviting with Christmas trees lighting up the windows, and the faint sound of carollers from nearby streets became the soundtrack to their journey.

Without thinking, William led them to his house. It looked just as it did in William's time. It was a little less wonky in places and the paint on the guttering was fresh. Still, it was home.

Except it wasn't – not then! Someone else lived there now, so there was no way William was going to be able to go inside.

'Er, this is me,' he said nervously as they slowed, then

stopped at the not-so-crooked gate.

Molly looked at the house. It was half the size of the rest of the houses in the street, but something about it felt inviting. 'It looks perfect.' She smiled. 'Cosy! Lucky you!'

'Yeah, it is. Well, it's a bit of a tight squeeze now that it's not just me and Dad.'

'Oh?' said Molly.

William paused. He couldn't tell her about her husband's future, but as she looked at him with her beautiful, kind eyes he just wanted to tell her everything.

'Now it's me, Dad, his new girlfriend and her daughter.'

'I see.' Molly smiled at him. 'Do you like her, your dad's new girlfriend?' she asked casually, leaning on the wall.

'Oh yes, Pamela's great! I mean, it's been a bit weird getting used to having more people living in our little house, and at first she hated Christmas so that's taken her a bit of time to get used to.'

'Hated Christmas? Remind me never to introduce her to the boy I'm meeting tonight. He'd do her head in!' said Molly, rolling her eyes.

'Yeah, he does!' William laughed. 'I mean, he would! *If* they were to meet . . .'

They both paused for a moment.

'Well, maybe next time you're finding your new family a bit strange, remember that she's probably finding it just as weird as you,' Molly said simply.

'I – I've never thought of it like that,' William said. And the more he thought about it, the more he realized it was true. He'd never stopped to wonder if Pamela ever found it hard to get used to their new life together, like he did.

'I suppose you'd better be getting inside. I imagine your dad and Pamela are very worried about you being out so late on Christmas Eve,' Molly said, nodding towards the front door.

William sighed as she swung the gate open for him.

'Merry Christmas . . . Wait, you didn't tell me your name,' Molly said.

'William,' he said with a smile.

'*William*,' she said. 'Lovely name.'

'Thanks for walking me home,' William said, and without thinking he opened his arms for a hug.

Molly didn't hesitate.

As her arms wrapped round him, William regretted pouring all the potion he'd found into the Christmasaurus's mouth: if he could, he would have stayed forever frozen in this moment.

But, like all the most wonderful things in life, it had to end.

As they pulled apart, William felt something fall out of his dressing-gown pocket and hit the pavement with a high-pitched *ding*!

'What's that?' Molly asked.

From the sound it made, he knew it couldn't have been the fluffy wish, and he started to wonder how on earth he was going to explain it if Santa's beliefometer had fallen out.

But, as Molly bent down to pick it up, William saw that it wasn't either of those things. It was the Winter Witch's frozen goblet.

Only it wasn't frozen any more. And he could now see that it was no longer a goblet either.

Perhaps it was the warmth of the beliefometer or the fluffiness of the wish, but, whatever the reason, the

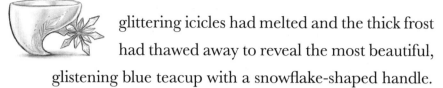

glittering icicles had melted and the thick frost had thawed away to reveal the most beautiful, glistening blue teacup with a snowflake-shaped handle.

William gasped.

He couldn't believe his eyes. It was exactly the same as the one that had belonged to his mother. The one that Pamela kept accidentally using!

'Wow, this is beautiful,' Molly said, admiring the pretty teacup in her hand. 'Whose is it?'

'Yours,' William said, without thinking.

'Mine?' She frowned.

William's heart raced. It was the truth. It was *her* teacup. He'd seen it in his kitchen throughout his life, watched his dad drink out of it sometimes when he felt lonely, and remembered how he couldn't bear to get rid of it.

'Yes. It's a Christmas present . . . from me – to you,' William told her.

'That's very sweet of you, but I couldn't possibly accept such a lovely thing,' Molly said, giving the teacup back to William.

'No, it's yours. I insist! Consider it a thank-you for

taking me home.' He smiled, and he knew he was doing the right thing.

Molly looked at the ornate cup in her hands.

'Well, if you're sure?'

'Absolutely!' William grinned.

'Then I'll think of you whenever I have a cup of tea,' she said with a smile, and William had never felt happier than he did at that very moment.

'Well, time to be off. Merry Christmas, William!' Molly gave him a little wave as she started to walk away.

'Merry Christmas . . .' William called after her. 'Mum.'

CHAPTER TWENTY-NINE
LOST IN TIME

William watched his mum disappear round the corner and his heart ached with happiness. It was a feeling he'd never experienced before, like he had somehow always been missing something that was now complete.

Suddenly a roar broke the silence of the night.

'Christmasaurus!' William gasped, remembering the crash. He moved as fast as he could back to the crash site, where he found long skidmarks that glittered with magic streaking across the road. They led all the way to the opposite pavement, where they disappeared through a big, messy gap in the green railings that fenced off his local park.

'Christmasaurus!' William called, and in an instant a roar answered him. He carefully entered the darkness of the park, and a few moments later found the Christmasaurus dragging the heavy sleigh out of the winter shrubbery with his teeth.

'There you are!' he said with a grin, and the Christmasaurus leapt over, covering William's face with slurps of affection. 'I'm OK . . . I'm OK!' He laughed. 'But . . . look at you!' The glowing light of the dinosaur's scales was now fading to the dimmest glimmer.

'Your brain freeze is wearing off,' William realized. 'And we still have one more town to deliver presents to. Then we have to find Brenda, and get her out of that swirly time stuff up there!' He pointed towards the bubbling storm clouds in the distance. 'We need to get out of here fast!'

As soon as William was safely in Santa's sleigh, the Christmasaurus slipped his head into the harness and dug his claws into the ground.

'Are you ready?' William called.

THE CHRISTMASAURUS AND THE WINTER WITCH

The Christmasaurus released an almighty roar.

'I believe in you!' William yelled, and the Christmasaurus sucked the cool air in through his nostrils and pulled as hard as he could across the snow-covered park. The glow of his scales became more intense as the brain freeze was recharged, giving him the energy to thunder over the frozen field, his steps becoming skips, his skips becoming leaps, his leaps getting longer and higher, until they were in the air once again.

'Yahoo!' William cheered. 'Now let's go and change the future!'

They zoomed across the clear Christmas Eve sky until they reached the first of the clouds where the storm opened up, allowing them inside. As they flew further into the storm, William realized that, with the Christmasaurus's scales glowing so brightly, he could guide the sleigh through the fog. It was as though the blue lights were a beacon showing him the way, just like the Winter Witch's eyes had done! As the clouds moved, he saw a moment appear. It was himself earlier that night, delivering presents to people's doorsteps.

Lost in Time

'That way!' William cried, and the Christmasaurus rocketed into the moment.

They were back in Christmas Eve. Time was slowly beginning to move, and there wasn't much of the night left before the children of the world woke and it would be too late! The storm clouds were brewing, claps of thundersnow boomed overhead, and bolts of lightning lit up the sky menacingly, as though the storm were ready to smother William and the Christmasaurus, to drag them back to their own time.

'Faster, Christmasaurus!' William screamed. As the sleigh shot onward, he loaded his arms with presents, ready to launch them on to the streets.

The sleigh suddenly burst into a brilliant red glow, as did the presents in William's arms, and the surrounding clouds were so close now that they too glowed with magical red.

'Quickly, down! Now!' he shouted to the gleaming Christmasaurus. They plummeted instantly to street level, and William threw the presents into front gardens, doorsteps, porches and balconies, showering homes with illuminated boxes of all shapes and sizes.

'One left!' William yelled, but the storm had closed in around them. A thick fog blanketed the last street and stretched out grey arms of mist, its wispy fingers ready to grab him. William leant out of the sleigh, the final present in his hand. The doorstep was approaching.

'Almost . . . there . . .'

POP!

The present fell out of his hand . . . landing neatly on the doorstep.

That very moment, they were consumed by the blizzard. Snow and wind, thunder and lightning, past and future, it all swirled around them. But they weren't interested in the past or the future now, nor were they worried about delivering toys.

The only present on William's mind was the one they'd left behind.

He opened his eyes as wide as he could, hoping they would *see* a way back, but the Christmasaurus's glow was dimming. He'd used up too much of his new power, and if they didn't make it back soon, they would be stuck in this storm, lost in time forever!

LOST IN TIME

Without warning, the sleigh jolted, not because it was blown by the wind but because someone had landed inside it.

'BRENDA?' William gasped.

She had returned, but she didn't look like the Brenda he knew. Time had transformed her. Her entire body was radiating a cool blue mist, and every inch of her skin was as crystal clear as ice.

She towered over William as she stood on the seat next to him with one foot resting on the front of the sleigh. She didn't look at him; her eyes remained focused ahead, and all of a sudden they emitted a beam of clear blue light.

'Follow that light!' William yelled, and the Christmasaurus pulled with all his strength, finding the power to fly faster than he'd ever flown before.

THE CHRISTMASAURUS AND THE WINTER WITCH

The Christmas Day sky shattered like a frozen pool as they burst into it.

'We're coming in too fast!' William cried, but there was no slowing them now. They crashed into the North Pole like a shiny blue meteorite, sending snow and ice into the sky as they hit the ground.

LOST IN TIME

Everything was white.

'Christmasaurus?' William coughed. 'Are you OK?'

The powdery snow-mist that hung in the air started to fade and, stuck in the wreck of the sleigh, William saw shadowy figures appearing all around.

**"William Trundle, is that you?
And was that Santa's sleigh you flew?'**

asked a series of melodic voices.

'ELVES!' William cried in delight. 'You exist again!'

The Christmasaurus suddenly popped his head out from underneath a pile of splintered sleigh wood.

'Christmasaurus! Look! We did it!' William cried, and the Christmasaurus let out a roar of celebration, as did all the elves as they untangled William from the wreckage, lifted him out and set him down in his wheelchair.

'Well, well, well, could that be the boy who saved the future I see before me?' came a deep, booming voice as a large figure stepped through the mist and engulfed them all in an enormous, warm hug.

'Santa!' William beamed. 'You're back!'

'Thanks to you, William!'

The Christmasaurus growled.

'Yes, you too!' Santa chuckled, patting him on the head.

Then William's smile dropped as he remembered who had saved them. 'Brenda! Where is she?' he asked, looking back at the bent golden metal and crumpled pieces of wood that were once the sleigh.

The elves exchanged puzzled glances.

> **'There's no one else, no Brenda Payne,**
> **Just you two crashed in Santa's sleigh,'**

Sprout and Starlump sang in a worried little melody.

The Christmasaurus roared as he sniffed something in the snow.

'Look, footprints!' William said. The Christmasaurus had found a trail that led away from the crash site, towards the Snow Ranch. 'It must be Brenda! We have to help her!'

The Christmasaurus put his head to the back of William's chair and pushed him faster than he could wheel himself, and they followed the trail of snowy footprints, with Santa and the elves not far behind. They wound their way back past Elfville, through the Snow Ranch, down the frosted hallway and the glass-panelled conservatory, and soon arrived at the entrance to the witch's maze.

'Don't stop!' William yelled, and tucked his head down just as they smashed their way through the first row of holly hedges.

Smash! Smash! Smash!

They cut a new path through the maze, all the way to the very heart, until they were in the frozen courtyard.

William stared up at the mysteriously magnificent ice sculpture standing over the fountain at the courtyard's centre. Her entire body radiated a cool blue mist, and every inch of her skin was as crystal clear as ice. Just like the very first time he'd seen her, William felt that there was something so familiar about her – as if they'd met before, long ago . . .

WAIT!

William's heart leapt in his chest.

Pieces of a puzzle he didn't even realize he'd been puzzling over clicked into place.

'What is it, William?' Santa asked.

'The Winter Witch. You said you didn't know who she was or how she got here,' he said.

'That's right,' Santa replied.

'Well, I think I know the answer,' William said, staring up into the frozen eyes of his stepsister.

'Brenda is the Winter Witch!'

CHAPTER THIRTY
A FORGOTTEN WISH

Though here was a sharp intake of breath as the surrounding crowd gasped in unison and looked to Santa for confirmation.

He nodded solemnly.

It was true!

'We have to save her!' William said.

'Save her quick, save her now!
Save the Winter Witch somehow!'

all the elves sang together.

'There has to be a way to bring her back!' William said. '*Back?* Back! I can go **back** in time and stop her from ever drinking that potion! It was too strong for her – look what happened!'

'**No!**' boomed Santa. 'William, don't you see? Brenda HAD to become the Winter Witch. If she hadn't, you wouldn't have followed her back and saved Christmas the way you did. It was meant to be this way!' He placed a comforting hand on William's shoulder.

Whether it was the weight of the hand or the weight of the moment, William suddenly felt like he couldn't take any more, and he did what anyone would do when there's nothing else they can do.

He cried.

As he cried, so too did the icy figure in the centre of the fountain, but Brenda's teardrops froze into icicles before they could roll off her frozen face.

'But she's my sister! I can't lose her!' William sobbed. He took a deep breath, trying to calm himself. 'I just *wish* all this ice would melt away and bring her back.'

Then, at those very words, something twitched inside William's dressing-gown pocket. A beam of warm white light emanated from within. The elves stepped back and watched in amazement as a tiny white ball of fluff floated out of the pocket and into the air.

'My wish!' William whispered.

In all the commotion, he had completely forgotten about the little magical creature that had stowed away in his pocket during their tour of the North Pole. 'Oh no – I promised I wouldn't make a wish . . .'

But the cute little wish-granting lump of festive fluff grew brighter and brighter, looking more magical and magnificent than William had ever seen it.

'William, you have just given that little wish the greatest gift of all. This chance to make your wish

come true is everything it has ever dreamed of,' Santa whispered reassuringly as they watched the light become a beautiful, festive shade of pine green. *A wish on behalf of someone else*, William remembered as his wish finally joined its fellow wishes in fulfilling its Christmas destiny.

Everyone watched with wonder as the tiny wish's light suddenly turned into a wave of warmth that poured over Brenda's frozen figure, melting away the ice from her head to her toes. The light intensified until the sky itself seemed as white as snow.

The Christmasaurus and the Winter Witch

The Winter Witch thawed . . .

. . . and her true form was restored.

'Brenda?' William said quietly as the light faded, and there she stood in front of the crowd, in the centre of the snowflake fountain.

'Well, it's about time!' she snapped, but a huge grin crept over her face as she climbed down and ran to give William the biggest hug.

'I never thought I'd say it, but I'm so glad to have you back!' he said.

'It happened so quickly and I couldn't stop it!' Brenda said. She screwed up her face, trying to remember. 'I was just so upset with my dad and angry with myself. The next thing I knew, I was skipping through frozen time, trying to unravel the mess I'd created. But . . . my brain was so frozen that it was like I wasn't even myself any more. Before I knew it, I'd been lost in time for what felt like forever. The only thought going through my mind was that I had to keep Christmas alive any way I could, to make up for what I'd done with that stupid bean.

'I went back to the very beginning of time, and every

Christmas Eve I made sure I froze time so that Santa could travel round the world, delivering presents. So the Winter Witch was born, and became part of Christmas legend.

'Over the years, I became so desperate to undo the wrongs of the silly, selfish girl I used to be that I became more Winter Witch than me. I forgot who I really was!'

'So, the tour of the North Pole – that was all your idea?' William asked, piecing the puzzle together. 'Not Brenda's, I mean . . . but the Winter Witch's idea?'

'Yes! I knew that was when this mess all started. But it was also how it needed to end. I had to bring us both here, so *I* could become the Winter Witch and show *you* the awful future I would create and what could happen to Christmas. Even my frozen, muddled mind knew that you were the right person to help save it. You and the Christmasaurus, that is!' she added, smiling at the dinosaur.

'You were pretty awesome, though, to be fair,' William said, giving her a nudge.

'Well, maybe next time you can try being frozen in time and see how you like it!' Brenda teased.

'I don't need to. I've got the Christmasaurus to freeze time for me!' William said with a smile.

The Christmasaurus stretched out his icy-blue spines with pride and gave them a shake, making them jingle like a wind-chime in a strong breeze.

'I do have one question though, Santa,' William said, causing a nervous expression to come over Santa's rosy face. 'We overheard you talking to the Winter Witch in the Forbid Den. Did you know this was going to happen all along?'

Santa took a deep breath, and everyone fell silent.

'Well, William, once Brenda became the Winter Witch, she could instantly exist throughout all time, crossing seamlessly from moment to moment. That's how she was able to be a part of Christmas in the North Pole for as long as me, and I've depended on her time-freezing power for many, many years,' he explained. 'But I always suspected that she had a greater purpose, that her reason for existing wasn't just to make my life easier on Christmas Eve – and I was right. She was there to save the future of Christmas itself. Well, once I knew this I had to help her, no matter what it took.'

'Even if it meant lying?' William asked.

'Well, technically I didn't lie. I just didn't tell you the truth,' Santa confessed.

'Sounds like a loophole to me,' Brenda said, placing her hands on her hips and looking sternly at him.

'Well . . . I suppose even Santa can be a bit naughty sometimes,' Santa admitted as his face flushed even redder than his coat. 'But you were never in danger, I can assure you of that. The Winter Witch had all time at her fingertips, and was able to try out every possible path, repeating Christmases over and over until she found a way – the only way – to save the future. She discovered that it was only this one very particular set of events that would get the job done. And you, William, were the only person who could do it.'

The Christmasaurus growled.

'All right, you too, Chrissy,' Santa added, patting him on the head.

'Ahem!'

Brenda coughed deliberately.

'Of course, you as well, Brenda! Each and every one

of us had to do everything we just did exactly the way we just did it, or Christmas would have been done and dusted!'

'So . . . you're saying that you knew this would all happen?' William asked.

'I knew as much as I needed to, William. Nothing more, nothing less,' Santa said.

'But did it work? Is Christmas safe again?' said William. They all looked at one another.

'Don't ask me!' Santa shrugged. 'I've only just started existing again!'

The Christmasaurus suddenly roared excitedly and ran through the hole in the hedge maze.

'I think he has an idea!' William said, and they all followed the giddy dinosaur. A few moments later, they caught up with him in the middle of Elfville, huddled over the TV. The hiss of static turned into voices as the Christmasaurus adjusted the pointy aerial with his teeth.

'There! That's it!' Brenda cried.

'**L**ook!'

She was pointing at the familiar smarmy features of her perma-tanned father, who could just be seen through the crowd that was waiting outside his toystore. The people made way, and William saw that he wasn't alone. Mr Payne was being escorted by two police officers, who practically dragged him to the police car by the collar of his tailored pinstripe jacket. They threw him in the back and slammed the door as Piers Snoregan's face came into shot.

'*Mr Barry Payne has been arrested over the millions of faulty Christmas presents he distributed around the world this December. One parent commented, "It would have completely ruined Christmas had my little Lily not woken up to find her real present from Santa sitting on the doorstep." One thing's for certain: Mr Barry Payne will be on the Naughty List for the foreseeable future. Here he comes now! Mr Payne, do you have any comment?*' Piers asked, holding his microphone out to the open back window of the police car as it went past.

Barry turned his head and looked straight at the camera.

'*I **hate** Christmas,*' he hissed through his perfect teeth as the car drove him away.

'*Some more breaking news,*' Piers announced. '*It appears Santa broke with tradition this year! Rather than leaving presents under the tree or in stockings, children woke to find them on doorsteps, in their front gardens and on porches and balconies. While people would traditionally be cooped up in their living rooms and kitchens, this new present-drop location has encouraged them to*

394

spend Christmas morning with their neighbours, sharing their gifts in what people are now calling the best Christmas since records began.'

Cheers erupted around the North Pole as William checked the beliefometer, which now showed a full jinglewatt reading.

'This really is the best Christmas ever!' he said, beaming.

'Actually, I saw one about twenty years in the future that was pretty good.' Brenda was smiling too.

'No spoilers!' said William with a laugh.

Once Snozzletrump, Specklehump, Sparklefoot, Sugarsnout, Snowcrumb, Spudcheeks, Starlump and Sprout had repaired the sleigh, and the ramp had been lowered, Santa, William and Brenda went aboard. The reindeer and the Christmasaurus were harnessed up, ready to fly, waiting for that extra bit of magic . . . the magic of music.

Santa placed a record on his golden gramophone and, as the opening bars of blasting trumpets played, the sleigh floated away from the snow, as if floating on the very notes themselves.

'**Off** we **go,** **ho, ho!**' Santa bellowed as they all waved goodbye to the hundreds of elves gathered below.

It wasn't long before Santa was carefully guiding the sleigh over William and Brenda's wonky little house. The street was alive with singing and dancing – the new delivery location had inspired a spontaneous Christmas street party – but luckily the neighbours were too full of merriness to notice the enormous sleigh, eight reindeer and blue dinosaur landing in the Trundles' back garden.

Bob and Pamela came running out instantly.

'SANTA!' Bob squeaked.

'Bob!' said Santa with a jolly nod. 'And merry Christmas, Pamela!'

'Where have you been?' Bob asked William.

'Not where, Dad – *when*!' William replied.

'And what about you? I thought you were with your father!' Pamela said to Brenda.

A Forgotten Wish

'It's OK. We'll explain everything inside. But now we can all spend Christmas together . . . as a family,' William said, and he saw Bob and Pamela flash each other a smile before squishing him in an embarrassingly squashy hug.

After a moment, Bob and Pamela released William from their arms, but found that he was still holding on tightly – not to Bob but to Pamela.

'Oh!' She chuckled with surprise. 'What's brought this on?'

'No reason – I'm just really glad you're here,' William said, and he caught Pamela glancing at Bob with a puzzled but happy smile.

'Well, now that I've delivered these two, I'd best be off,' Santa boomed, patting Bob on the back so hard he nearly fell over.

Santa hopped into the sleigh while Brenda and William said their goodbyes to the Christmasaurus.

'Thanks again, Chrissy. I owe you!' Brenda said, and the Christmasaurus gave her face a big, sloppy lick. She stepped away, leaving William and the Christmasaurus alone.

'Well, another year over, another adventure.' William smiled. 'Same time next year?'

The Christmasaurus put his head to the sky and replied with an excited roar.

Santa picked up the reins as the sleigh floated off the ground and slowly started to glide forward over the Trundles' garden.

'**Santa!**' William called. 'Without the Winter Witch next year, how are you going to freeze time to deliver all the presents in one night?'

Santa smiled.

'Well, although the side effects of freezing time are disastrous for humans, it appears that some other creatures can cope with the power of brain freeze a little better. William, thanks to you, I think we might have found a new job for a certain, very special dinosaur . . .'

The Christmasaurus roared with pride from his spot at the front of the sleigh, as his icy scales glowed subtly with the remnants of the winter magic.

William grinned. 'Who needs a Winter Witch when you've got a Christmasaurus!'

A Forgotten Wish

'Brenda,' Santa called down, 'I must say –'

'– thank you for all the years of time-freezing assistance I gave you as the Winter Witch? You're welcome!' Brenda interrupted.

'How did you know I was going to say that?'

'I've been to the future, remember!'

Santa chuckled. 'Yes, well, you have more than earned your place back on the Nice List. If there's anything you want for Christmas . . .'

'It's OK, Santa. I know now that I don't need any more wishes or presents. I've got everything I could ever want right here,' Brenda said as she reached into her pocket and pulled out the beautiful snow globe that Bob had given her to remind her of home.

'*Family*,' she said with a smile as the snow fell on the little log cabin inside.

William looked at the beautiful ornament and his heart filled with warmth as he realized that somewhere out there, across time, his mum was with him, and would be forever.

As he sat between his smiling dad who had his arm round Pamela, and his new sister Brenda, who was gazing

happily at their wonky little house, William realized that this might just beat last year as the best Christmas ever.

And, with that, Santa, the sleigh, the reindeer and one very special dinosaur disappeared into the December sky.

THE END

ACKNOWLEDGEMENTS

It's that time of year again . . . No, not Christmas! It's time to write my acknowledgements! You may have noticed my name sprawled across the front and down the spine of this book in a rather large font, which does wonders for my ego but doesn't in any way represent the hard work of so many people who have contributed their talents to get these pages into your hands (or file on your ebook reader).

So, here I shall attempt to remember as many of those people as possible and hope that these small splodges of ink on the page (or pixels on the screen) in the shape of their name make them feel all happy-tingly.

The Christmasaurus and the Winter Witch

Let's start with the man responsible for the magical illustrations that bring my words to life in ways that I could never have imagined: Shane Devries. It wouldn't be Christmas(aurus) without you.

That leads nicely on to the person who introduced me to Shane: Michael Gracey. Once again, your imagination and ideas have been so brilliant and inspiring. Thanks for pushing me to do better!

Of course, I wouldn't know either of the above people without Fletch, who has managed me for eighteen years! None of anything I've ever done would have happened without you. Thanks, Fletch.

Tom Weldon and Francesca Dow, who allow me to keep writing these books, to conceive overly elaborate announcement videos and generally to be what I imagine is a rather difficult author, thanks for your continued belief and patience!

On to the wonderful wintry witches at Penguin Random House (and by *witch* I mean the beautiful, ice-sculpture kind, not green, spotty ones with cats . . . although some of them may have cats): Amanda Punter, Lauren Hyett, Sonia Razvi, Hannah Sidorjak,

ACKNOWLEDGEMENTS

Sophia Smith, Emily Smyth, Mandy Norman, Wendy Shakespeare (and her editorial elves Jane Tait, Sophie Nelson and Marcus Fletcher), Eliza Walsh, Sarah Roscoe, Becki Wells, Zosia Knopp, Maeve Banham, Susanne Evans, Aurelie Goncalves and Toni Budden. You are all so brilliant and I can't thank you enough.

Natalie Doherty, I feel like you got the short straw when the giant Penguin was deciding who would be my editor, while I, on the other hand, won the lottery and got you! You are the absolute best and I could not write these books without you . . . quite literally. Thank you!

Stephanie Thwaites, aside from being the best agent in the publishing universe, you always manage to say exactly what I need to hear at just the right time. Thanks for putting up with me and all the drama that comes with me!

David Spearing, thanks for your directorial wizardry on all the announcement videos and content around this book and for generally being a great, inspiring friend! Also, a shout-out to Raff and all the teams who always bring their A-game to those vids.

Nikki Garner and Tommy J. Smith, you two are always

405

there for me, making the impossible happen on the tightest of deadlines. I'm so lucky to have you two in my life!

Thanks to the brilliant Whizz-Kidz for once again helping make William Trundle a character who will hopefully inspire wheelchair users and children with disabilities around the world, and to Inclusive Minds for their brilliant thoughts and input.

Mum and Dad for the childhood Christmases that ultimately led me to write these books and for watching my kids while I write them!

Carrie (who's singing at the top of her voice upstairs as I write this) for being annoyingly talented and inspiring.

Giovanna, for accepting me and my Christmas obsession and for allowing Christmas songs to be played outside December . . . occasionally in July.

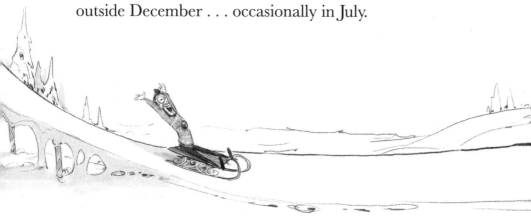

ACKNOWLEDGEMENTS

Thanks to Buzz, Buddy and Max, my three little elves who have given Christmas, and life, a whole new meaning.

Finally, to anyone and everyone who has read this book, I just wrote the words; it was your mind that brought them to life. Thank you.

ABOUT Whizz-Kidz

move a life forward

The story of Whizz-Kidz started with a bloke in a bike shop.

It was 1989, and our founder, Mike Dickson, was at work in his shop when he saw a girl in a wheelchair looking up at a bike light on the shelf above her. Mike asked if he could help, but the girl politely replied, 'No thanks, I can reach it myself,' pushed a button on her powered wheelchair and rose up to pick the light off the shelf.

It was at that moment that Mike understood the difference the right wheelchair can make to a child's life. Because to that little girl, that small action – getting something off a high shelf – meant something far bigger. It meant independence.

Mike set out to run the London Marathon and raise enough money to pay for a single powered wheelchair for a child who needed it. By the time he crossed the finish line, he'd raised £9,000 for a girl with cerebral palsy. One year later, Whizz-Kidz was born.

Since then, Whizz-Kidz has transformed the lives of more than 20,000 disabled children, providing them with life-changing mobility equipment to give them the best possible start in life.

Today, we do so much more than providing equipment to young disabled people; our youth clubs, wheelchair skills training, residential camps and work placements each contribute to helping young disabled people make friends, have fun, learn life skills and, ultimately, achieve their true potential.

We still have a long way to go, and many thousands of children are still waiting for the right equipment to give them freedom, independence and hope. But we are extremely proud of all we have achieved, and we are incredibly grateful to all of our supporters – including Tom – who have made our achievements possible.

Together, we'll continue working to achieve our vision that all disabled children's lives are full of fun, friendship and hope for an independent future. Just like any other kid's. **www.whizz-kidz.org.uk**

Dear Santa,

It's me, Tom, your favourite Nice Lister here! Well, it's that time of year once again and I'm ready to write my Christmas list. Some people think I'm too old to write to you and, sure, I look and act like a grumpy thirty-four-year-old man sometimes, but we both know that's not the real me, and deep inside I just want to play video games, eat sweets all day and sleep until 11 a.m., but I've got to at least pretend to be a grown-up from time to time.

Anyway, here's my Christmas countdown of the ten things I would like this year. They might not be things that can be wrapped up under the tree or found inside a stocking, but Christmas wouldn't be Christmas without them . . .

10 **Roast potatoes!** Crispy, crunchy, golden and munchy. They are the highlight of Christmas dinner, the star of the show, the headline act! In fact, I'd go as far as saying forget the turkey, ditch the sprouts, fling the pigs-in-blankets, give me a whopping bowl of roast spuds and I'll be a happy customer.

9 **Christmas movies.** I couldn't even begin to name my favourite, but we all know it's not Christmas unless you've got a funny festive film on in the background while you gather with the family and play . . .

8 **Christmas games.** It's not Christmas Day unless there's a sticky note on your forehead with a famous name written on it while you strain your brain to figure out who you are, as your family laugh and take the opportunity to eat . . .

7 Nibbles! Nuts, dates, chocolates, cheese, mince pies . . . Nom, nom, nom! (And a marshmallow-stuffed winter coat would be nice . . . then I could have nibbles when I'm out and about!)

6 Songs! This might be the best thing about Christmas (apart from roast potatoes). 'Last Christmas', 'Wonderful Christmastime', 'All I Want for Christmas Is You' . . . If you can only bring me one thing from my list, this might be it. Maybe throw in a roast spud on the side, though.

5 Christmas pud! OK, I know I banged on about the potatoes earlier, but you can have roast potatoes every week. Christmas pudding comes once a year (unless you're my nan, who has an unlimited supply in the cupboard . . . just in case). I'm not a pudding snob – shove it in the microwave for a few minutes and whack a tub of cream on top and wake me up when the *Doctor Who* special starts.

4 **Early morning.** Forget the alarm clock . . . I've got three kids. They wake me up before 6 a.m. all year round (thanks, guys), but Christmas Day is the one day of the year I'm happy to get up before them. Nothing beats that moment when you wake up and realize IT'S CHRISTMAS!

3 **Decorations.** OK, so you might need to pop down my chimney a little early if you're going to bring me some of these, as I like to put mine up mid November. Too early for some, but I just can't wait for December the first. Plus, my grinchy wife likes to take them down before the New Year (I know!) so I have to get in early if I'm going to maximize tree time!

2 **Advent calendar.** What better way to start your day than by opening a hidden door and munching on some chocolate? You might have to speak to my mum as she still buys me mine and I don't want to be greedy and end up with two!

1 **Happiness.** OK, this isn't something you can wrap up in a box or leave in my stocking, but the truth is, I don't really want toys or gadgets – I don't need stuff. All I want is for my family and friends to be happy at Christmas; if they're happy, *I* will be too. And what more could you want for Christmas . . .

Wait, a dinosaur! I should have asked for a dinosaur! Oh well, there's always next year . . .

Merry Christmas, Santa!

Tom
X

Now you can listen to William's adventure too!

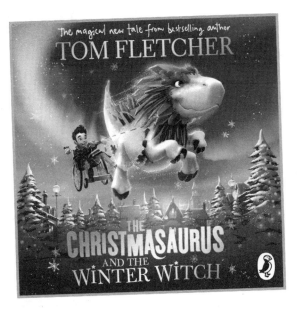

Have you read William's first adventure?

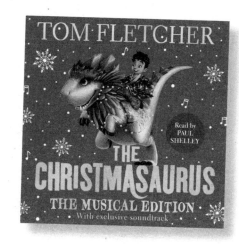

Have you ever wondered what's really under your bed . . . ?

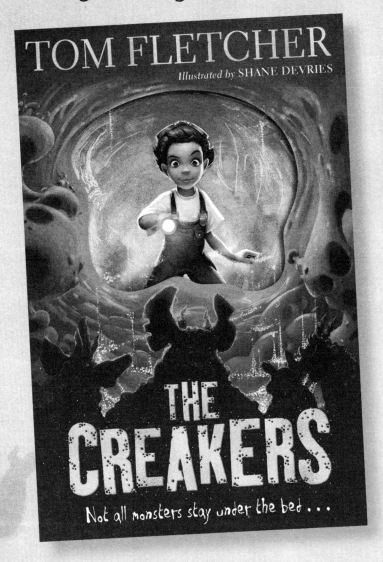

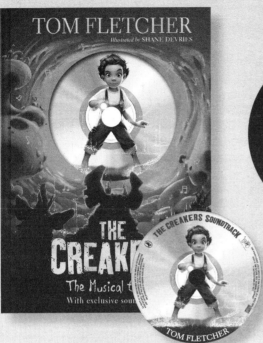

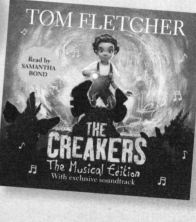